Snow Globes and Hand Grenades

a novel

KEVIN KILLEEN

Blank Slate Press | St. Louis, MO

Copyright © 2015 Kevin Killeen
All rights reserved.
Published by Blank Slate Press
an imprint of Amphorae Publishing Group
4168 Hartford Street, St. Louis, MO 63116

Cover design Kristina Blank Makansi
Interior design by Kristina Blank Makansi
Cover art: Adobe Stock

Library of Congress Control Number: 2015954929

ISBN: 9781943075126

PRINTED IN THE UNITED STATES OF AMERICA

To our daughter Emily, who, when she was in eighth grade, sneaked off with my laptop and read the only two chapters I had of this story. "Dad, you should finish that," she said. "That's the kinda book I would read."

Snow Globes and Hand Grenades

FOREWARD

SO WHAT ARE YOU DOING?

You should be out in the sun getting some fresh air, not reading this book.

But here you are.

I can see you standing in the aisle of a used bookstore years from now. Maybe it's cold out and you're just killing time. This book has been long out of print. The author died broke and mumbling.

What kind of fool book was this? Was there any heart? Was there anything real? It even smells musty.

This was a novel about the last two weeks of eighth grade at a Catholic school in mid-America in the spring of 1973. People always asked me, "How much of that stuff really happened?"

I'll tell you the truth.

It was a great time to be a liar. Nixon was in the White House. The nuns ran the school I went to. And we were always in trouble. We were always facing some interrogation by the police or the parish leaders. It usually went like this:

"Did you do it?"

"No sir."

You could feel your blood pounding in your veins, because you really did do it. You could also feel the weight of all your sins piling up on your chest.

God was recording every word you were saying, but you had to lie with a straight face. There was great honor in lying well, in outsmarting the adults.

Under such pressure deep friendships and romances were formed. It went on like that for years, the boys in their khaki pants, the girls in their plaid skirts, all young and becoming.

And then the last bell rang and everyone left. Just like that. Eight years of criminal joy and fellowship swept away. Your friends went to high school, college, got married, moved to other towns. The teachers—kind and cruel— retired, disappeared, and then turned up on the obituary pages. How could that be? How could all those boys and girls trooping down the hallways in their parochial uniforms have marched off? What was then the present moment seemed as solid as the school cornerstone. But it turned out to be a flimsy thing to lean on. Little is left of those last two weeks of eighth grade, except the class picture, a boy's white cotton shirt with his classmate's signatures on the back from the final day—and these following pages.

If you must read on, please, read outside where you can get some sunshine and fresh air.

- Kevin Killeen

CHAPTER 1

"WHAT THE HELL?" Mimi Maloney said, squinting into the sun. There was something strange about Mary, the gold statue on the church roof, and Mimi wasn't the only one who saw it. As a crowd gathered, some began to point.

It was Mother's Day, and the archbishop in his flowing purple robe had just spoken from the pulpit. "Yours is a model parish," he said. "The children so well-behaved, the adults so devout." Walking out the front door of the church, the archbishop saw the commotion and looked up for himself.

"What in heaven's name?" he said whipping off his sunglasses.

Something was sitting in Mary's hand, something glinting in the sun that wasn't there before. Under orders to investigate, a heavy-set usher ran panting up the steps to the choir loft, cut through the storage closet, and climbed through the trap door onto the roof. Standing on the highest peak, the usher looked like a miniature man in a dark suit beside a giant gold woman. The crowd on the lawn watched. An old man pinched his itchy nostrils. A new mom holding a baby squeezed his milk bottle so hard that formula shot out, spraying the archbishop and several startled lay persons. Mimi got it in the eye.

"Be careful," someone shouted at the usher as he stretched farther and farther, higher and higher, longer and longer until he finally snatched something from Mary's grip. After climbing down and retracing his steps, he bolted out the front door, and handed the object to the archbishop. Everyone leaned forward to see what it was. The archbishop turned it this way and that, but there was no getting around the fact that it was a snow globe paperweight with the words "Visit Colorado" stamped on its base. Snowy particles suspended in water swirled about a mountaintop with skiers descending on a romantic village. Without saying a word, the archbishop handed it to the usher, got in the back seat of his waiting car, and sped off.

"What does it all mean?" moaned a Mothers' Club member.

It meant that the missing snow globe someone had stolen a few days earlier from Miss Kleinschmidt's classroom had been found. A stern, cigarette-thin woman who'd been teaching eighth grade for decades, Miss Kleinschmidt was given to outbursts over sloppy handwriting and boys with un-tucked shirts. Her fondness for the Visit Colorado snow globe had driven someone to swipe it, and it's discovery in Mary's outstretched palm touched off an Inquisition that would burn through the final weeks of school.

On Monday morning, Miss Kleinschmidt slammed the door and faced her class. "Whoever is responsible for this scandal, this sacrilege," she said rubbing her arthritic knuckles, "will find his Catholic high school acceptance letter rescinded."

Sara Jibbs, one of the nicest girls in class who never did anything wrong, raised her hand.

"What!?" Miss Kleinschmidt snapped.

"What's that word mean, rescinded?"

Miss Kleinschmidt clapped her hands together as if popping a child's birthday balloon. "It means taken away, torn up, no longer yours. It means even though you think you've been accepted, the gates will be barred and you won't be let in." She paced up and down the aisles, smacking her dry tongue off the roof of her mouth and looking around at the boys. "Whoever did this, will find his future scuttled in the opium den of the public school system."

As Miss Kleinschmidt wheezed on and on, Patrick Cantwell stole a glance at Tony Vivamano, his best friend, and then stared out the window at the green grass of their last spring at Mary Queen of Our Hearts grade school. Patrick looked guilty. And so did Tony.

CHAPTER 2

MIMI HOPPED on her green Schwinn with a white basket between the handlebars and rode off the school playground. She stopped on the golf course where she thought no one was watching and took off all her clothes down to her white underwear.

"Hey, what's that?" said Tony, who was down the fairway with Patrick. They had stopped on their way home to discuss the snow globe crisis and were lying on the thick grass watching the clouds drift across the sky. "Holy crap, Patrick, look!"

Patrick rolled from his back to his stomach and blinked. With her hands on her hips, chin up and her bobbed brown hair breezing above her shoulders, Mimi faced the sun like a statute of flesh and freckles.

"That's Mimi Maloney. What's she doing?" The boys lay silent on the grass next to their bikes and waited for her next move. Mimi reached into a bag in her bike basket and pulled out a green blouse. She slipped it over her head, buttoned it up, and then pulled out a red plaid skirt and stepped into it. It was a Catholic high school uniform, the kind the older girls wore at Holy Footsteps Academy, an all girls prep school. Mimi picked up her grade school clothes and stuffed them in the bag. Then she got on her bike and pedaled away.

Tony squinted in thought and looked at Patrick. "Her house is the other way. Where do you think she's going?"

"I have no idea," Patrick said. Without another word, they got on their bikes and followed her, careful to keep their distance.

Mimi knew exactly where she was going. She'd been planning her trip to Holy Footsteps Academy for weeks. Her mission was to sneak in and steal a blank sheet of school stationery from the office. She planned to take it home to type an official letter to her parents informing them that her earlier acceptance to Holy Footsteps was a mistake—and that Mimi should attend Webster High instead.

Mimi was sure her plan would work. It had to work. She was in love. She was in love with a public school boy from Webster High and was determined to pedal her bike forward toward a future of her own choosing.

By the pond at the edge of Holy Footsteps Academy, the boys stopped to watch Mimi lean her bike against a tree and run in the front door. "What's she up to?" Patrick said.

"I don't know, but whatever it is, I think I'm in love," Tony said. "Let's follow her in."

"No, wait. What about our plan? We have to decide."

Their plan, which was really only Patrick's plan, was to hop a freight train and run away. He'd been dreaming about it for years. Living near the Missouri Pacific train tracks and seeing hobos all the time, he too, wanted a future of his own choosing. He wanted to ride the rails away from the future others had planned for him—high school, college, marriage, working downtown—and let his legs dangle out of a slow boxcar as he passed through other towns, other states, and wide open farm country with no nuns.

In fifth grade he'd been home sick with the croup the day five friends got caught smoking on the kindergarten roof. They ran away from the principal's office, busting out the door to spend hours on the loose. The Gang of Five had lived off the land, swiping candy bars from the Tom Boy in Glendale, hiding out on the Interstate 44 construction zone, and evading an hours-long search by concerned parents and police. Their freedom, though it only lasted for six hours, gave them the honor, respect, and self-confidence no school desk ever could. Having missed that day sick at home coughing was a failure that still stung. And now the snow globe crisis had given him his last best chance to have a good reason to run away, but only if Tony could see the good in it and join him. Freedom was fine, but only if you had a friend to share it with.

"Maybe we could run away," Tony said, his voice full of hesitation "But let's see what Mimi's up to first."

Mimi's footsteps lighted catlike across the front hallway, over polished floors, past dark woodwork, and through dust particles dancing in the afternoon sun. Her head was down so no nun would notice she was a stranger. She could hear the muffled notes of nuns lecturing and smell the old books with doodles in the margins from girls long graduated whose daughters were now doodling. Up ahead was the office with its milk glass door showing the dark shape of nuns moving about to process tuition invoices. Mimi stopped.

A nun burst from a storage closet across the hall carrying a fresh spool of calculator paper to tabulate the incoming checks.

"You there! What are you doing out of class?" the nun said, "Come here."

Mimi flinched, but kept her head down and itched her forehead to hide her eyes. "Sorry, Sister, it's my period. Gotta go." She ran around a corner and up a flight of steps, leaping three steps at a time, hoping to reach the landing and get around the corner before the nun would reach the bottom of the stairs and see her. Heart pounding, she stopped on the next floor to listen. Nothing. The nun had walked on to the office.

Meanwhile, out by the pond, where the lazy tips of a weeping willow teased the top of the water, Patrick and Tony talked about the church investigation.

"We can either run away before they find out or after," Patrick said, "Maybe I should just turn myself in and tell the truth."

"Never tell the truth when God wants you to lie,"Tony said watching the school for some sign of Mimi. "It's in the Bible."

"Really? Where?"

"Lots of places."

"Like where?"

Tony picked up a big rock to stall for time and threw it in the water with a splash. "I got it. Samson."

"Who?"

"You know, the muscle guy. When he lied about his hair, he was fine. But as soon as he told the truth, they had him."

Mimi pulled her hair back into a ponytail as she tiptoed past a drinking fountain and along a hallway lined with lockers. She spied her destination in the distance: the fire alarm with its bright red paint and big white letters screaming at her to "PULL." That was her goal—to pull the fire alarm and dart into a nearby restroom while the rest of the school emptied out. She stopped short of a classroom full of senior girls listening to a nun read romance literature. Mimi's cold fingers reached toward the fire alarm while the nun paced back and forth and the girls' crossed legs bobbed beneath their desks.

"Let him kiss me with the kiss of his mouth," read the nun with no makeup, "for thy breasts are better than wine, smelling sweet of the best ointments. Thy name is as oil poured out; therefore young maidens have loved thee…"

The alarm clanged. The nun's head whipped up from her book. Mimi ran.

Out by the pond, Patrick and Tony were skipping rocks to see who could get one to the island first when they heard it. They watched as lines of girls in red plaid uniforms skirts led by nuns in black habits filed out of the doors onto the lawn.

"Must be a drill,"Tony said. Then his eyes widened and he turned toward Patrick.

"No way! Did she do it?" Patrick said. "But why?"

Tony blew an Italian kiss toward the school, hoping it wound find her. "I don't know, but if she did, God, I love her even more."

Mimi peeked out into the hallway. The last girls were going down the stairs. She stole out into the open, dashed for the staircase, and bounded down toward the first floor.

She skidded to a halt next to a white statute of Pope Pious XII and spied around the corner as the last nuns left the office, scurrying out the front door. Mimi was alone. She owned the school. Running into the principal's office, she opened desk drawers looking for the letterhead. Pens, caramels, and broken rosary beads cluttered the main drawer. She tried another one, rooting around beneath a browning banana. Slamming that drawer, she opened another and there it was—a stack of virgin white official Holy Footsteps Academy letterhead with matching envelopes. She grabbed two of each, folding the paper to fit in the envelopes, stuffed them in her blouse and ran out a side door into some bushes just as the fire truck arrived, siren wailing. Waiting for the next part of her plan to fall into place, she watched as the firemen in their yellow hats ran into the school.

Then it happened.

Though Mimi could barely hear it over the fire alarm still blaring inside, the class bell rang, signaling the end of the school day, and the girls of Holy Footsteps Academy broke formation as if on command. Laughing, chatting, and ignoring the nuns hollering at them, they headed toward carpool moms waiting in station wagons lined up down the street. For all they knew, their school would be burned to the ground by tomorrow, but the girls didn't care. It was time to go home for Ding Dongs and Twinkies. Mimi blended into the crowd, got on her bike, and rode away with a determined look on her face. She rode right past the pond where Patrick and Tony studied her from behind a tree.

"What do you think it's all about?" Patrick said.

"I don't know, but I'm definitely in love."

CHAPTER 3

MISS KLEINSCHMIDT bought her first and only bottle of hair color the night before she went to Colorado, the trip where she met a man on the slopes. She had seen the brochures of young couples smiling and hugging in wool sweaters, huddled around crackling hearth fires, and imagined herself in one of the pictures. The man she met was handsome, with thick black hair, a good build, and a winning smile. He knew how to poke the fire and keep the conversation going. The snow swirled outside the lodge window while Miss Kleinschmidt and her man were inside. She had just brushed her teeth. He held her in his arms and kissed her. They made love. She felt young and alive and forgot her schoolroom of eighth graders. But the trip came to an end, and the man bought her the snow globe at the lodge gift shop and hugged her goodbye.

There were some letters at first, mostly from her, but then he dropped out of touch, and Miss Kleinschmidt let her hair turn gray. The snow globe had been sitting on the shelf for decades, a reminder of her bitter disappointment and a stark warning to never again embrace such foolishness. She dusted it off from time to time and shook it to make the snow swirl. Then with a death-like gurgle, she would hack up some phlegm from the back of her throat, only to swallow it back down, and put the snow globe back on the shelf.

The day Patrick stole the snow globe began like any other. It was Monday, May 7, just a few weeks before graduation. Miss Kleinschmidt stood at the front of the class.

"Today in history," she began, munching on a soda cracker like she did every morning. It was her custom to eat soda crackers while talking about all the grim things that had happened on that particular day, thereby instilling in her students a respect of ruin and calamity. She would stand behind her desk wearing one of her gray, tan, or harvest gold pants suits and launch into some tragedy of the past—battles, deaths and plagues seemed to be her favorites.

"On May 7, 1840 a tornado hit Natchez, Mississippi, killing three hundred and seventeen people. What do you think of that?" She looked out the window at what was a sunny day in St. Louis. "I guess we'll be all right today," she shrugged, sounding a little disappointed. "Oh well, time to turn in your papers on *The Scarlet Letter*."

Now in her seventies, she reached out a skeletal arm to take each student's paper. Her gray hair, highlighted by the fluorescent ceiling lights, looked like a giant Brillo Pad floating above the crowd in the Macy's Day Parade. Fingerprints and makeup particles smudged her round wire-frame glasses, obviously not cleaned for days. A greasy silver chain drooped from her glasses frame and looped around her neck, swinging as she walked. But as she stalked the rows of desks, it was her breath that signaled her presence—a dry-mouthed paste of cigarettes, crackers, and the piping hot black coffee she gulped in the teacher's lounge. She couldn't catch anyone unawares.

Patrick watched her stop at Tony's desk. He knew Tony didn't have the paper to turn in because they had talked about it on the way to school.

"I had a bad weekend," Tony said as they climbed the church lawn under the gold statute of Mary. Tony's brand new—and only—girlfriend since fifth grade had broken up with him. And she didn't even tell him herself. It was a remote control breakup, the worst kind. Another girl who was friends with her gave him the bad news.

The phone call had come on Sunday afternoon as Tony watched his dad carry Brando, the family beagle, out to the car and place him in the back seat. "She just doesn't like you," the friend had said as Tony's dad pulled out of the driveway and headed to the veterinarian to have Brando put to sleep. Brando was old, nearly crippled with arthritis, and had lost most of his teeth and all his bladder control. Tony loved that dog. He hung up the phone and spent the rest of the afternoon watching a Clint Eastwood western while eating a quart of Bryer's peach ice cream right out of the paper box. All the shooting and horse galloping seemed to comfort him, some. He fell asleep hugging a pillow that smelled of Brando and never even started *The Scarlet Letter*.

"Mr. Vivamano, where is your paper?" said Miss Kleinschmidt.

Everyone in class looked up to hear his answer. Tony whispered something about his dog.

"What's that? Speak up!"

"My dog died," Tony said in a voice that cracked with puberty and sorrow.

"Do you honestly expect me to believe that your dog's ill health stretched out over the entire four weeks you had to read this book and prepare a two-page report?"

Tony hung his head and mumbled something about how the dog had been feeling poorly for several weeks.

Something about Tony's answer triggered the eruption. Miss Kleinschmidt drew in a deep breath and then exhaled slowly, a noxious fume filling the air around Tony's head. "Look at all these papers. The other students managed to find the time." She rolled up the other papers she'd collected and whacked her open palm.

"Look at me. They all answered my assignment. They cared enough. Don't you care? Do you think you can get through life with your thick black hair, and your muscles, and your winning smile?"

"No, ma'am," Tony said, keeping his head buried in his arms on his desk.

"That's right!" she thundered. "It's not too late for your grades to collapse and for me to send a letter to that fancy high school you've been accepted to. They can still change their minds." With that, she shot a glance at Patrick and a few other known coasters.

"That goes for all of you!" She smacked the roll of papers on Tony's desk. "Now get up and go to the boy's room and wash the shame off your face. Maybe when you come out, you can act like a man."

Tony's nostrils flared like someone in a Clint Eastwood movie planning to blow up a bank. He pushed his chair back and stood, wiping hot tears from his red face as he headed for the hallway. Everyone else handed in their papers, and Miss Kleinschmidt shuffled through them at her desk, clearing phlegm from her throat now and then to show disapproval.

When the final bell rang, she went to the teacher's lounge to have a cigarette. All the students were gone—all except Patrick. That's when he stole the snow globe for Tony. At least, that's how it had started. Mrs. Kleinschmidt had been cruel to his friend, and now he was going to pay her back. But as Patrick reached out to pick it up, he thought of all the trouble stealing the snow globe could cause. He remembered the Gang of Five and how they got in trouble, so much trouble that they ran away. He picked up the snow globe and saw the white flakes swirl around the tiny romantic village. Maybe stealing it could get him—and Tony—in so much trouble they'd have to run away. He could picture them watching the countryside roll by from inside a boxcar. So, he grabbed it and ran down the hallway and outside the school. There he saw Tony's bike by the church steps. He pulled the heavy door open and crept into the cool dark. Inside, he found Tony sitting in the shadows of a back pew.

"This will teach her!" Patrick said handing Tony the snow globe.

"I don't want it." Tony had been half thinking, half praying, and wasn't really in the mood for criminal activity.

But Patrick kept pushing it. "Follow me," he said, and led Tony to the choir loft, through the storage closet, and up through the trap door. When they got up on the church roof, they looked down on the school building, and Patrick started in about how grade school would soon be over, but then how another four-year sentence waited for them in high school. Then college and a job downtown. Marriage. Kids. Gray hair. Death. Patrick looked down at the pavement and imagined the shattered snow globe being discovered after morning Mass. He imagined getting caught, being expelled, going free. He wound up his throwing arm.

"Wait!" Tony said. He took the snow globe from Patrick and climbed up to the peak of the roof alone.

"What are you doing?" Patrick called up, "Don't fall."

Tony rested the snow globe in Mary's right hand. Her thumb was open, so the glass sphere fit snugly in her grasp as if she had been waiting for it all along. He climbed back down to Patrick's level and caught his breath. Brushing off his hands, he looked up to admire his work.

"What'd you do that for?" Patrick asked.

"Let her deal with it."

CHAPTER 4

THE HAND GRENADE was displayed on a shelf in the den behind the leather chair where Mimi's father sat in his red plaid underwear lecturing her about the future. The reading lamp beside him threw a corporate shine on his bald head, white legs, and black executive socks, and at the end of each sentence, he pointed at her the way his boss had pointed at him for years.

"Now, you've got to understand," he said, raising his voice so he could be heard over the Chopin concerto Mimi's high school sister was playing on the upright piano in the living room, "my promotion will mean a level of security this family has never known. I've worked very hard for it, just as your sister has worked hard to get straight A's at Holy Footsteps. Why, listen to her play."

Mimi listened to a few notes and nodded. Her eyes wandered to the hand grenade. A souvenir from the Korean War, it had a wire twisted tightly around it and through the eye of the pin so no one could ever fool around with it and blow up the house.

"Here you go," said Mrs. Maloney, breezing into the room wearing an apron with fresh pot roast stains. Three safety pins were pressed between her lips, and she carried her husband's new suit pants over her arm.

"Hey, Mom," yelled Mimi's sister while she played the concerto, where's my other uniform?"

"I put it in your drawer, dear," Mrs. Maloney called out.

"No you didn't. It wasn't there."

"Look again. You'll find it. It couldn't have just walked off on its own." Mrs. Maloney smiled admiringly at her husband and handed him his new pants.

Mr. Maloney stood and thanked her with an executive nod, then turning to Mimi, he continued his presentation as he shot his legs into the pants to try them on. "This party we're hosting for the boss and some of the office staff is important," he said. "Everyone must say and do just the right thing. We don't want them to rescind the promotion."

"Oh, don't say that." Mrs. Maloney laughed and waved her hand at her husband as if batting away an invisible fly. "They can't rescind something they've already authorized."

Everyone turned as Mimi's brother burst into the den dribbling a basketball on a patch of hardwood floor between the Persian rugs. He was wearing his CYC select team uniform and gym shoes, rifling the ball between his legs and spinning it on his finger.

"Look at you, only in the fifth grade and already a pro," Mr. Maloney said. "You'll end up with a basketball scholarship someday."

"Cool," Mimi's brother said and spun the ball faster.

"Take that outside," Mrs. Maloney said. "Your father is getting his uniform fitted for the promotion party."

"Do you have to wear a uniform for your new job?"

Mr. Maloney laughed. "No, son, I don't have to. I get to. Now, go outside and shoot some baskets. You want to stay sharp."

"Yes sir," Mimi's brother said as he took off running through the living room toward some future basket.

Mr. Maloney sucked in his stomach and buttoned the pants. He zipped up and patted his ribs. "After seventeen years with the company," he said to himself.

"Hold still, dear," Mrs. Maloney said, crouching at his feet to safety pin his pants legs for alteration.

Mimi looked at the clock. "Can I go now?" she asked. She didn't want to be late for her secret phone call with her boyfriend. "I have homework."

"Homework?" her father said. "I'm glad to hear you say the word. All right, you can go. And by the way, don't mention your grades at the party.

The boss's daughter is also going to Holy Footsteps next fall, and I hear she's getting straight A's. No reason for you to feel any … less than her. As long as you've been accepted, that's all that counts."

"What if they change their minds for some reason?" Mimi said. She was thinking of the fake letter that was coming.

"Oh, don't say that," Mrs. Maloney laughed.

"That's right. You're in," Mr. Maloney said. "Holy Footsteps, and then college. We can afford that now. You've got a real future all of a sudden."

Mimi sighed and tried to sound happy. "Thanks, Dad." She got up to go upstairs when her mother called out, "And don't forget to brush your teeth, and throw your dirty clothes down the clothes chute and straighten up your room and…"

With her mother's voice fading in the crescendo of the Chopin concerto, Mimi reached the top of the stairs at precisely nine o'clock. The antique clock chimed, and she lifted the hallway princess phone off the hook and dialed Time and Temperature. Then she stretched the cord into her room to close the door and sat on her bed with the phone to her ear.

"Thank you for calling Community Federal Time and Temperature," the recording said. Mimi started breathing faster. By dialing Time and Temperature, no one else in the house would hear the phone ring when her public school boyfriend called. The Maloney's had the new Call Waiting system. All Mimi had to do was wait for the beep-beep, then click over to get the incoming call in secret. That's what she had been doing for months and she hadn't been caught yet. But lately—for the past nine days to be exact—there was nothing to get caught about. For some reason her boyfriend had stopped calling. Maybe tonight was the night. Yes, she could feel it. Tonight, he was going to call again and apologize and tell her he loved her. She could feel that phone call coming. He was probably dialing right now. She waited and listened for the beep-beep to interrupt the Time and Temperature recording.

"Do you need a loan for an engagement ring? At Community Federal, we can help…"

But there was no beep-beep. She felt her eyes getting wet as she looked around the room at her unmade bed, the Almond Joy wrapper, the pile of 45s by her Close and Play record player, the *Seventeen* Magazine on the floor, the cluttered desk with a brass lamp shining on the black typewriter she had used to type the fake letter from Holy Footsteps Academy. She grabbed the letter from under her pillow eager to read it to her boyfriend, like a love letter.

> Dear Mr. and Mrs. Maloney,
> We are writing to let you know your daughter can't come to our school after all. It seems we admitted too many girls and won't be able to fit them all in our classrooms. It would be too crowded and your daughter wouldn't be happy or able to learn right. The good news is we have checked with Webster High School, which is a really good school for girls and boys, and they have plenty of extra desks on hand. We know that Mimi will enjoy her high school years there and save you a lot of money you would have spent with us on tuition. Thanks for understanding, and please don't call us about this, because everyone is very busy at this time and our decision is final.
> Sincerely,
> Sister Jeanne Flourie, Principal
> Holy Footsteps Academy

The Time and Temperature recording got near the end. "The time is 9:01. Downtown temperature 66 degrees—"

Beep-beep.

Mimi's heart leapt. She drew in a joyful breath and pressed the button to click over to her boyfriend.

"Hello?" she whispered.

"Mimi? Is this Mimi Maloney?"

"Yeah, who's this?"

"This is Patrick Cantwell, from school."

"Patrick Cantwell? Look, I'm expecting a call. What's up?"

"Oh, I'm sorry. It's just that I have this friend … and well, he likes you."

There was a hundred-year silence on the line. Mimi stuffed her fake letter under her pillow and pointed her finger at the phone the way her dad had pointed at her. "That's nice of you to call. But you've got to understand, somebody else already likes me. I can't go with anybody else, ever."

Patrick looked for some crack of light, for Tony's sake. "Ever? You mean, forever, ever?"

Mimi hesitated, but then whispered out sharply, "That's right. Look, I gotta go."

"OK, well, first, though, don't you at least want to know who the guy is who likes you? He really cares about you all around, as a person. Don't you want to know who?"

There was another hundred-year silence on the line.

"Hello?" Patrick said.

"OK, who?"

He told her it was Tony Vivamano and she burst out laughing, and then all Patrick heard was a dial tone.

CHAPTER 5

A POLICE CAR AND A BLACK VW BEETLE arrived outside the school. It was early the next morning. Detective Sergeant Kirk Kurtz, a man with neatly trimmed nostril hairs, was behind the wheel of the police car. Kurtz had a list of unsolved juvenile crimes in the area, similar in style to the snow globe incident. The VW was driven by Father Clive Ernst, a devout member of the Archdiocese special investigations committee who had just last Christmas cracked the case of the three wise men stolen from St. James parish. This was a powerful alliance of church and state. Together they were determined to not only catch the snow globe perpetrator, but to also extract confessions and put an end to the wave of juvenile anarchy around Mary Queen of Our Hearts. Patrick and Tony walked whistling across the church lawn, not yet noticing the two cars parked by the school flagpole.

"I don't know about Mimi," Patrick said, "Maybe she's holding us back from our own future."

"Women take time, believe me. Anyway, thanks for calling her for me," Tony said. "You're my best friend at this rock pile."

"You're welcome," Patrick said, his voice skipping like a record with guilt he hoped Tony didn't notice. He hoped Tony didn't realize that he too was also attracted to her. And how could he not be? After seeing Mimi in her underwear and watching her sneak into a high school and run out during a fire alarm? She had a lot of good qualities. Before yesterday Mimi was just an average girl, but now she stood apart from all the other girls in vivid Technicolor. Only for Patrick, she was even more vivid. He was the one who had called her on the phone and heard her voice—even heard her laugh.

Patrick looked at Tony and thought about their friendship, all the good they'd accomplished together since they met in fifth grade. They had been fired together as altar boys, rolled the dumpster down the playground hill into the fence, made a UFO out of two pie tins with a string attached and hovered it from a tree branch by Father Maligan's window, captured a rabbit and let it go inside the cafeteria, set off fire hydrants near the homes of girls they liked, and even done some homework together.

"Maybe you should call her next, not me," Patrick said.

"No, I trust you. You'll know what to say. Hey, look!"

They both spotted the police car with the officer standing by it and the priest in a long black trench coat slamming his door. They knew right away what it was all about and stopped dead on the hillside.

"The snow globe!" Patrick whispered."

"Who else did you tell about it?"

"Nobody."

"That's good. Just remember, God is on our side, and if you have to, lie about everything."

They shook on it and went inside to take their seats in Miss Kleinschmidt's classroom. Patrick wondered if this would be the day he and Tony would finally get into some real trouble and get to head for the tracks.

CHAPTER 6

PATRICK SAT AT HIS DESK relaxing with a paperback about bank robber John Dillinger, while Tony read *The Scarlet Letter* to prepare for writing a late book report. Mimi picked at her fingernails and wondered why her public school boyfriend hadn't called for so long. What was he doing right now? Was he thinking of her? Did he still love her? She looked up at Miss Kleinschmidt and wondered if she had ever been in love. Not likely, Mimi thought. Who would love someone as mean as her?

The whole class held a grudge against Miss Kleinschmidt. Earlier that month, she had promised to let them go to the zoo for the spring field trip. But on the day of the trip, a blooming May morning, she rescinded the offer. "Your scores on the science test were abysmal," she told the class. "Some of you don't even know all the planets." That's when she turned to Tony in the front row and used him as an example. "Mr. Vivamano, you could only name Earth, Pluto, the moon, and the sun, two of which aren't even planets."

Tony hung his head and Miss Kleinschmidt kept after him. "Do you expect to just waltz into that prep school ... where is it you're accepted?"

"St. Aloysius," Tony said.

"That's it, St. Aloysius. You expect to just waltz in there on the first day of high school, knowing you're on earth, but not knowing the rest of the planets?"

"I'll never leave earth," Tony said shrugging.

She smacked her hand on his desk. "You'll never leave *here* until you know the solar system. Tell me, if you can, what's the temperature of the sun? Where is it hottest?"

"July?"

Everyone sunk down in their desks and unzipped their windbreakers for a full review of the solar system. By the end of the morning, every kid in the eighth grade knew that the hottest part of the sun was the core, that it's twenty-seven million degrees Fahrenheit, and every kid wished Miss Kleinschmidt was there.

Miss Kleinschmidt hadn't given another thought to canceling the zoo trip. She'd been preoccupied with following the news about President Nixon, and this morning was no different. She had her head buried in the newspaper reading an article about how Nixon said he had "no knowledge" of burglars breaking into Democratic Party headquarters at the Watergate Hotel when there was a knock at the door. She placed her newspaper on the desk and stood as all the students looked up.

It was Father Ernst and Detective Kurtz. Even as they greeted Miss Kleinschmidt, they studied the eyes of the students as if trying to sift their very souls from a distance. Patrick marked the page on his Dillinger book and turned it upside down on his desk.

"Class, these two men are here to help us," Miss Kleinschmidt said, coughing up a glob of phlegm, then swallowing it back down. She nodded at the priest and he stepped forward as she retreated to the back of the classroom.

Father Ernst was a tall, thin man with high cheekbones, short black hair and brown bulging eyes. Those eyes! They looked out at the class like the eyes on a church statue, when the air smells of burning candles and you remember about the money you stole, or the curse words you said, or the lie you told your mother. And then he spoke. His voice was even worse. His voice was deep and arresting like a sudden sermon.

"In 1917, the Virgin Mary appeared to three shepherd children in Fatima, Italy," he began. "Is anyone familiar with this miracle? Please raise your hand."

No hands were raised.

"The Blessed Mother showed them many wonderful things, many

secrets, but first, she showed them what was at the center of the earth, and do you know what it was?"

No one knew.

Father Ernst walked up and down the rows of desks with his black leather trench coat resting on his shoulders and flowing behind him like a cape. "It was a burning lake of fire and it was full of bad people, people flailing and screaming in agony, people with no hope for all of eternity." He paused by Patrick's desk, reached out and turned over the paperback. A low *hmm* rumbled from the base of his throat, and then he put the book down and kept walking. "As Miss Kleinschmidt told you, we are here to help you because we care about your future. Both of us care about you."

Father Ernst looked toward the front of the class, where Detective Kurtz stood at attention in his blue uniform shirt with a shiny badge. He was a shorter man whose face was red with determination and high blood pressure. On his belt was a holstered pistol and shiny handcuffs. Kurtz patted his gun, then ran his hand across his bristly, gray crew cut. He was sure that someone in this very class was involved in the snow globe incident—and that that someone was probably also involved with the wave of crimes he was determined to solve. He took a breath and reached over Miss Kleinschmidt's desk for the snow globe.

"Careful!" she blurted out from the back of the room.

Detective Kurtz nodded to her, and slowly picked up the snow globe. Snowflakes swirled between his fat, pink hands, and Mimi, as if hypnotized by the scene, was transported to the night she met her pubic school boyfriend on the golf course. Snow was falling steadily and the fairways glowed a soft bluish white. The hills were crowded with children sledding. There was laughter and danger and no adult supervision. An older boy smiled at her and invited her to share his sled. Before she realized he was a non-Catholic, they were racing down suicide hill, walking and talking, warming themselves by the fire and feeling each other's steamy breath on their cold faces. He held her hand. She smiled. Without warning, he kissed her. It was a quick, confident, public-school kiss that opened a bank vault of emotions Mimi never knew she had on deposit.

"This stolen snow globe represents just one of the crimes I'm interested in," Detective Kurtz told the class. He put the snow globe down randomly on Mimi's desk and she watched the snowflakes fall as he continued.

"There have been too many acts of vandalism in this area. One of you must know something. It's my job to catch the bad boys who are doing these things and see that they are punished."

Miss Kleinschmidt walked up, snatching the snow globe from Mimi's desk. Mimi's tear ducts burned.

"I've already warned them that whoever is responsible for this will have their Catholic high school acceptance rescinded," she said. Miss Kleinschmidt held the snow globe tight in her hands and looked at the detective and priest for approval.

"We'll take it from here, ma'am," Detective Kurtz said.

"To finish," Father Ernst interjected, his voice booming from the back of the room, "we want to give you a chance today to make a good confession." He walked to the front of the class with his black cape trailing and stood alongside Detective Kurtz and Miss Kleinschmidt. He cleared his throat dramatically. "If anyone here wants to clear his conscience today, let him simply raise his hand and admit that he took the snow globe and put it in Mary's hand."

Patrick and Tony's palms got sweaty. Blood pumped through their temples. The room was quiet except for the tick of the clock and the buzz of the overhead florescent lights. No one moved. Seconds went by. The priest and the detective narrowed their eyes and studied the faces of the boys, gauging for any signs of nervousness or concealed guilt. Then a hand shot up.

It was Mimi.

All eyes turned to her.

Detective Kurtz cocked back his neck in surprise. So the culprit was a girl! He got out a pen and paper to write down the girl's name. Then, overcome by his feelings for Mimi, and the memory of her white underwear shining brightly in the afternoon sun, Tony raised his hand. Patrick's heart raced. This was it. Tony was in trouble. Big trouble. The big day had finally arrived. He closed his eyes and raised his hand, thinking of boxcars rolling across barley fields. But while Patrick's eyes were closed, another boy raised his hand. He raised it because Miss Kleinschmidt had once told him not to sign his name so fancy, with so many loops. Two girls whom Miss Kleinschmidt had called "hussies" for wearing slightly shorter uniform skirts also raised their hands. A boy she once scolded for falling asleep during a planetary slide show raised his hand. Left and right, up and down the aisles, students who had endured months of her bad breath and constant carping shot their hands into the air. It was an avalanche of confessions. It was the best the class had felt since she canceled their field trip to the zoo. When Patrick opened his eyes, he saw that every single student in the class had a hand raised.

The priest and detective and Miss Kleinschmidt looked at each other.

"So, if everyone was involved," Detective Kurtz said, "then everyone will face questioning." His face was even redder than before and he clicked his ballpoint pen like a gunshot.

At that, everyone dropped their hands, and realized they were all in trouble. Mimi was the last to lower her hand.

"We will talk to you one on one," said Father Ernst. His voice was calm but sorrowful. "I know the Blessed Mother will be watching over our proceedings to ensure we arrive at the truth." Father Ernst and Detective Kurtz marched out of the room.

Miss Kleinschmidt put her snow globe back on the shelf and the sweat mark from her angry palm evaporated.

CHAPTER 7

SISTER MATHILDA, the last nun at Mary Queen of Our Hearts to wear a black habit, had been forced into retirement and was recovering from cataract surgery. Parish authorities had decided to put her in a nursing home for nuns, as soon as she healed from the surgery. But Sister Mathilda had her own plans for the future, which she had shared with no one. Wearing taped-on black eye patches and a harness attached by a wire to a dog run line in the back yard of the nunnery, she paced and plotted. Her plan was to get her vision back and then drive away in the Cutlass Supreme she had won in the 1966 school raffle.

She walked back and forth smelling the flowers, listening to the birds and the children coming out for recess onto the playground, and thinking about her car which was parked alongside the nunnery, the keys safe inside a waterproof rosary pouch and hidden under a rock by the little kindergarten house. Most of the students ignored her as she walked in the nunnery yard. She was the most forgotten soul in Purgatory to them. Others, mostly young boys, would come by to tease her and throw sticks at her, hoping to make her mad so she would blindly chase them. But the only reaction they got was a blessing and a request to please describe what the spring day looked like. No kid ever did. They just laughed and ran back to the playground.

"Please pray for me," she would call out.

Patrick and Tony and Mimi and all the class walked out the side doors and down the steps onto the playground. The white stone school, three stories tall, was sunlit against a blue sky. Boys in khaki pants, white shirts, and blue ties, and girls in blue and green plaid skirts, ran the bases playing kickball. The older boys and girls stood talking in the shade along the chain link fence, where an overhanging maple tree dropped helicopter seeds that twirled to the blacktop pavement. Tony chased a falling helicopter seed trying to catch one before it landed. He snagged it in his palm and laughed.

"What are you doing?" Patrick said.

"I was just pretending," Tony said with a deep breath. "If I can catch this, we won't get in any real trouble from all this crap."

Patrick took the helicopter seed from his hand and flicked it on the ground. "Why'd you raise your hand?"

"When I saw Mimi do it, I had to."

They looked down the fence line at Mimi. She was surrounded by the other eighth grade girls, just like the photo in the newspaper of President Nixon surrounded by reporters.

"Did you really do it? When did you do it? How'd you get on the roof?" the girls shouted.

Mimi shrugged. The approval of her classmates meant nothing to her because she had her public high school boyfriend. She had the fake letter in her book bag ready to be dropped in the mail. She had her own future ahead with him at Webster High. She deflected the questions with questions of her own.

"Do you think I did it? How do you think I did it?"

"C'mon, Mimi, tell us. We raised our hands, too."

The boys gathered around Tony and Patrick, because they were the first guys to raise their hands.

"So, Tony, what kind of shit have you got us into? Did you do it?"

"I'm telling you the truth," Tony said lying, keeping one eye on Mimi down the way, "I don't know who did it, but I just raised my hand for the hell of it."

They turned to Patrick and asked him the same question. He glanced at

Tony, and then also lied. "I don't know why I raised my hand. I don't know anything anymore."

The boys and girls debated amongst themselves, guessing and whispering and asking each other who did it. The general feeling was that either some of the first ones who raised their hands really did do it, or nobody in Miss Kleinschmidt's class did it. Maybe it was a student from long ago who hated her and broke into the school at night. Maybe it was the janitor. Maybe it was Miss Kleinschmidt herself. Maybe she had finally gone crazy and climbed up to the roof just to have one last thing to hold over them all.

They looked up to the window of the teacher's lounge. There was a gap in the venetian blinds and somebody swore that it looked like Miss Kleinschmidt was up there spying on them, trying to figure out who did it.

She was, of course. But she couldn't figure it out. Not yet. Nobody was patted on the back. No one was lifted up on the shoulders of the crowd as the hero. There were no clues. But she knew the guilty one was on the playground right before her eyes. She just couldn't tell yet who it was.

The bell rang and the kids headed back inside. Sister Mathilda paced back and forth with the dog-run line trailing behind her, blind to the world, biding her time.

CHAPTER 8

PRESIDENT NIXON STRUGGLED to concentrate on his work in the Oval Office, but the thought of the approaching Senate hearings on Watergate was too distracting. He rubbed his temples and considered the facts. He knew he was guilty. He had lied and denied any knowledge of the caper. In fact, he knew all about the Watergate break in and he knew about a wave of other crime his operatives had carried out—things that might come out if they could pin him for Watergate. He tossed down his pen and changed into his tennis outfit for a game of ping pong in the White House basement with Chinese ping pong master Feng Lu.

Feng had been on retainer for some time, going back to the days before Nixon's historic visit to China. He spoke no English and at age ninety was stone deaf, so Nixon could curse or sing the Navy song or talk about national security matters with visitors without asking Feng to leave the room. Nixon was sweating profusely, bobbing around the table in his white knee socks, white tennis shoes, and white shorts and shirt. Feng breathed calmly, fielding the ball with deft movements, as he stood at the center of the board wearing his grey one-piece jump suit. Nixon felt he was gaining ground against Feng when Henry Kissinger appeared carrying some important papers.

"So *zeese* is where you are," Kissinger said sounding annoyed as he ducked to avoid bumping his head on a ceiling pipe.

"Henry!" Nixon said, slicing his paddle through the air to give the ball some spin, "I've decided everything's going to be fine."

"Oh?" Kissinger said as Feng returned the ball with a gentle under thrust that caused it to land on the far right corner of the table.

Nixon dove for the ball, smacking it with all the anger he felt toward the journalists, Democrats, and anti-war demonstrators who had fomented this season of upheaval. Feng held his paddle by his side and waited as the ball rocketed out of bounds and into an adjacent laundry room, where the President's black socks were oscillating. Nixon tripped over the ping pong table leg, and toppled to the floor.

"Meester President," Kissinger sighed as he helped Nixon up, "You must consider how this situation could affect your future ... even your presidency."

"Horsefeathers!" Nixon said with a renewed determination. "I'm the only one in charge of my future. You'll see. They'll all see." He pointed at his opponent with his paddle. "Right, Feng Lu?"

Feng nodded in deaf agreement and got out another ball to serve.

"You just keep our allies on board and the world will see that old Dick Nixon can still play ball," the President said. "But if you're really that concerned, drop by after dinner and we'll discuss it. Pat's making lemon pie."

"I'm sorry, Mr. President. I have another commitment this evening."

"What, another date?"

Kissinger looked at the floor. "Yes, Mr. President."

Nixon shook his head. "Henry, you're a smart man. Tell me, why are you always falling in love?"

"I don't know. I can't understand it myself, sir."

Nixon motioned for Kissinger to leave the papers on a side table and went back to his game. Feng could see Nixon was tiring, so he eased up and let him win.

CHAPTER 9

TONY AND PATRICK washed Chips Ahoy cookies down with cold root beer and watched a rerun of *Gilligan's Island*. They agreed it was a stupid show, but liked having it on for the sake of Ginger and Mary Ann. Tony had invited Patrick over after school to help him fake out a report on *The Scarlet Letter*, but Patrick wasn't much help. He had based his report on the back cover and on the article in the World Book Encyclopedia. "You're not supposed to use the encyclopedia for reports," Tony said, "They can tell."

"Not if you use synonyms," Patrick said.

"How's that work?"

"You know, if the encyclopedia says Hester was 'depressed', you just say Hester was … 'suicidal'."

"Was she?"

"I don't know, but that's what I put down."

The front door opened and Tony's older brother Vince came in from high school. He was a sophomore at St. Aloysius, the all boys Jesuit prep school where Tony and Patrick had been accepted. Vince had thick, black wavy hair like Tony, and muscles. He carried a heavy book bag full of homework like it was nothing.

"Hey, Vince," Tony called out from the TV room.

Vince didn't say anything but walked to the edge of the TV room, glancing at the Chips Ahoy bag, the root beers, and the *Gilligan's Island* rerun. "What, no homework?"

"Oh, we're working on it right now," Tony said reaching for a piece of loose-leaf paper with the first paragraph of his report. The paper had been on the couch earlier, but had fallen to the floor unnoticed. He picked it up. "Yeah, we're working on a book report. Nothing big."

Vince cast an indicting look at Patrick.

"We've got it all outlined in our heads," Patrick said.

Vince put down his book bag on the chair, then got out all his fat textbooks to show the boys the homework he had as a sophomore at St. Aloysius. It was about two hours worth of work before dinner, he said, and then more reading after dinner, and a paper to write before bed. "I don't think you guys realize what's expected of you," he said. "If you want to make it, you can't be watching *Gilligan's Island*."

Tony and Patrick looked at each other, then at the TV. The Skipper was hitting Gilligan on his head with his cap because Gilligan had ruined another chance to get off the island.

"Is it really that hard?" Patrick asked.

"It's like lifting weights." Vince made a muscle with his arm, which was quite well developed, because on top of all his homework, he lifted bar bells. He was a straight "A" student with dates on the weekend and plans for the future.

"I got muscles, too," Tony said, rolling off the couch onto the floor to do push ups. Patrick and Vince watched him do about ten and then he farted and collapsed to the floor laughing.

"Go ahead and laugh," Vince said. "But it won't be funny, if you don't exercise your mind. Your mind is like a muscle and it can go flabby." Vince went into the kitchen to eat some grapes and a banana, and drink a glass of milk to power up his mind for homework.

Tony rolled over on his back to see the TV better, and Patrick leaned back on the couch to consider the future. A fresh rerun of *Petticoat Junction* was starting. The boys didn't say anything as the soothing theme song invited them to spend the next half-hour with Bobbie Jo, Billie Jo, and Betty Jo. They made sure to pay special attention to the part where the three sisters were in the water tank taking a bath.

"What are we gonna do about Mimi?" Tony sighed.

"I don't know," Patrick said.

"Maybe you should call her and tell her I raised my hand first. Tell her I raised my hand first after her."

"What good'll that do?"

"I don't know. Girls like to be rescued. Don't they?"

"I don't know."

Tony was watching *Petticoat Junction*, thinking. "Just call her tonight, okay?"

"You should call her. She's your girlfriend."

"I can't bear another breakup."

CHAPTER 10

MIMI BIT HER LIP and flopped face down on her bed so no one could hear her cry. Downstairs, a houseful of adults were laughing and talking at her Dad's promotion party, while upstairs she gripped the princess phone like a vise, her thumb pressed down hard on the hang-up button. She couldn't believe it. Her boyfriend wanted to break up. After all this time of being in love! This time she had called him to tell him to meet her on the golf course right away. She wanted him to know the truth—that other boys liked her, and that one of them had just called her. It was only Patrick who'd called, but still.

"Hello," Patrick had said, "I'm calling about someone who really likes you."

"Who is this?"

"It's Patrick Cantwell again, from school. Tony and me were talking—"

She had almost hung up, but stopped. What if she could show her boyfriend that other boys liked her? What if her boyfriend could see Tony walking up to meet her on the golf course? Maybe he would be jealous. Maybe then he would start calling her again.

"So, Tony, he really likes me?" she asked.

"Oh, who wouldn't? I mean, yeah, Tony, he likes you," Patrick said.

"Well, why don't you have him come talk with me on the golf course?"

"Really? Just meet you there some night?"

"Yeah, tonight, right now. By the pond by Suicide Hill."

"What? You mean right now?"

"Sure, why not? I'll be there in a few minutes. I gotta make a quick call." She hung up and called her boyfriend, which she'd never done before. She thought she'd be nervous, but she wasn't. She was confident now that another boy liked her, too. Her boyfriend's mom, a woman with a loud, nasally voice, picked up on the second ring.

"Skiiiiiiiiiiiip," she yelled, "it's your girlfriend again."

Again? Mimi's stomach tightened. Why would she say again? This was the first time she had ever called.

"Hello?" Skip said sounding eager.

"Skip?"

"Who's this?"

"It's Mimi," she said with a dry throat whisper.

"Uh … Mimi … um … hi…."

"Yeah, look," she said clearing her throat, "I have to see you right away. Can you meet me on the golf course?"

There was a long pause and she could hear the TV in the background. "I don't know. We're watching *Hawaii Five O*, and it's right at the good part."

"Skip, I have to see you."

He cleared his throat and told her the facts. "Mimi, I've been meaning to call you. I don't know if we really have … a future together."

"What?"

"I think its best that we—"

"WHAT?" She grabbed the closest thing, a tube of Clearasil, and hurled it across the room where it plunked against the window pane and fell into her white wicker trash basket. "You can't do this!"

"I think its best, you know?"

"You can't break up now, not now. I mailed the letter today."

"The letter? What letter?"

"You know, the letter I told you I was going to write from Holy Footsteps to my parents, so I could go to Webster."

"You really did that? I forgot about that." He sounded like he still trying to watch *Hawaii Five O* while he talked to her.

"I did it for us," she said.

"Us? Well, look, Mimi—" He tried to break up with her some more. He was gentle about it, but Mimi kept interrupting and yelling, "Not over the phone, not over the phone!" So he agreed to meet her in a few minutes on the golf course by Suicide Hill to tell her to her face.

Mimi wiped her face with the back of her hand, got off the bed, hung up the phone, washed her face, and put on her pink windbreaker. Her head was swirling as she descended the burgundy-carpeted staircase. She had to leave right away, but casually, without calling any attention to herself. Mimi's sister sat at the piano under the brass sheet music light in her Holy Footsteps Academy uniform. She was playing Chopin's "Nocturne Number Two in E Flat Major" like it was nothing. Her Dad's boss sat on the living room couch in a dark suit and tie with a Dutch Master cigar in his fat hand. Blue smoke hung above the end table lamp. All the adults had mixed drinks and the men wore loosened ties from the office. Their wives, in light spring dresses and adorned with perfume and jewelry, sat in the corner by a plastic potted plant. The boss was telling the men exactly what the baseball Cardinals needed to do with their pitching this year, pointing at them with his cigar at the end of each sentence like it was part of his punctuation. The men nodded in agreement.

"Where are you going?" Mimi's mom asked her.

Mimi stopped. "Oh, nowhere. Just out to get some air."

"Out to get some air? She's probably got a date," said one of the wives smoking a Virginia Slim cigarette.

Mimi froze.

They all laughed at her.

"Not my Mimi," her mom said swallowing some bourbon and water. "She's been accepted to Holy Footsteps Academy, the all girls school. She's too smart for boys."

The Virginia Slim lady toasted her. "To Mimi, the smartest girl at the party." The wives all raised their glasses to Mimi, looked at their husbands, and laughed.

"Well, at least put on some proper shoes. You can't go out like that." Mimi looked down at her feet and noticed they were bare. "You left your shoes in the den, honey."

Mimi tiptoed into the den. Her younger brother was playing tabletop hockey against a group of junior executives and beating them. She saw her sneakers on the floor by her dad's chair and slipped into them. He can't break up with me, she told herself. It will ruin everything. But what could she say to make him change his mind? She glanced at the junior executives who moaned in unison when her brother won another point, and then at the neatly folded *Wall Street Journal* on her dad's chair, and then up at the shelf behind the chair. There it was. The hand grenade. It was dark green and oval like a fat egg with a flat bottom and square bumps all over it. She looked around. No one was watching her. The room was dim, except for the orange, leaded glass light above the game table. Her brother scored another a goal, manipulating the sliding rods to pass the puck from the right wing to the center and flick it in the net. One of the junior executives shrugged in defeat while the others slugged back their Old Fashions. Mimi reached up and took the hand grenade and slipped it into her windbreaker pocket.

Through Chopin notes and adult laughter, Mimi's footsteps were silent as she crossed the Persian rug into living room. She cut through the kitchen and out the back door. The storm door banged behind her and she was free. Walking alone under a streetlight, she got out the hand grenade and studied it. "He can't break up with me, not now," she mumbled. Her fingers unwound the grenade's safety wire, wire that had been twisted tight since her Dad had returned home from Korea. She dropped the wire on the grass and headed towards the golf course. The night air was soft with spring and moonlight, the kind of night Chopin wrote songs about.

CHAPTER 11

"THIS IS GONNA BE GREAT!" Tony said as he and Patrick walked toward the train tracks that separated the neighborhood from the golf course.

"Something must've changed," Patrick said, "but I don't know what."

Patrick scuffed along in the same battered Keds, blue jeans, and faded plaid shirt he'd had on after school, even though, at the last minute, he'd combed his hair and brushed his teeth. The blood pulsing through his veins made him a little light headed, and as they reached the tracks he paused and let his gaze follow the gleaming rails down into the distance, the same rails that should be carrying him and Tony away to freedom. And then he kept on going, tagging along with Tony to be near Mimi.

Mimi, Mimi, Mimi. The thought of her propelled them both forward.

"It was probably me raising my hand that changed her mind," Tony said, adjusting the buttons of his gold paisley shirt with white wing collars. He'd left the top three buttons undone to show off his chest. There was no hair yet, but Tony wasn't waiting.

"I don't know. She sits in front of you. How could she see you?"

Tony stopped to cup his hands in front of his mouth and smell his breath. "One thing, we have to promise."

"What?"

"If she tries to kiss me and thank me and tell me she loves me—"

"Yeah?"

"Don't let me tell her anything about the snow globe. That has to remain top secret."

"I know."

"We have to keep that secret no matter what, or somehow it will get out."

"You're right."

"God, if only I could tell her I put the snow globe up there, she would probably want to stick her tongue in my mouth. How's my breath?" Tony leaned forward and breathed on Patrick. It smelled of toothpaste over spaghetti.

"It's okay."

"I drank a lot of water after you called." Tony ran his hands around his waist to make sure his shirt was tucked into his skintight brown bell bottoms and adjusted the galloping horse's head belt buckle. "Water always helps."

As they left the tracks behind them, they headed down the middle of the fairway, Tony's polished brown disco boots leaving a trail of shallow heel prints in the grass. The air smelled of wet grass, warm mud, and honeysuckle—and growing things that promised the school year was almost dead. Up ahead was the hill once crowded with kids sledding. But the winter was forgotten. Suicide Hill was desolate.

"I think I see her."

Mimi came out of the tall, arching creek tunnel that ran under the train tracks onto the golf course. The creek was low and she had walked through the tunnel in the dark, staying to the sides where the creek bed was dry. The boys could see she had on a pink windbreaker and bellbottom blue jeans, and her hair was breezy. Tony waved to her. She waved back and climbed out of the creek onto the fairway. The boys walked up to her. In the moonlight, they could all see each other's faces plainly. It was quiet.

"Hi," she said, keeping her hands in her windbreaker pockets.

"How's it going?" Tony said.

"Good."

That's all she said, kind of blankly, too, so Patrick jumped in. "Mimi, you know Tony, don't you?"

"Sure." She nodded to him and looked around for her boyfriend. The putting green at the bottom of Suicide Hill was empty. The water on the pond ruffled from the wind.

"It sure was brave of you to raise your hand today," Tony said, fixing his hair a little. His hair was as wavy as chocolate cake frosting, and he knew that all girls loved chocolate.

She shrugged and looked around some more. Inside her windbreaker pocket, her right hand was wrapped around the grenade. Her palm was sweaty.

"I don't know if you could see in class," Patrick said, "but right after you raised your hand, Tony raised his hand … so you wouldn't be in trouble alone. He was the first one."

Mimi looked Tony in the eyes for the first time. His eyes were brown and lonely; hers were green and sad. For a second she felt guilty using Tony to get her boyfriend jealous. But she blinked and steeled herself for what was coming. "Thanks," she said.

"You're welcome," Tony said, looking at her pink lips.

A train horn blew down the line, a freight charging down the tracks. They turned in that direction and could see the headlight sculpting the green baby leaves on the trees that stood along the tracks. The passing engines sent out a vibration across the landscape that went right through them. "I have to go see a man about a horse," Tony said stepping away.

"What? Where's he going?" Mimi said.

"He'll be right back. He just drank a lot of water."

Mimi nodded. Patrick looked at her. She was watching the train like she had a lot on her mind. Patrick thought about the other day, Mimi standing sharp against the blue sky in her white underwear; about earlier tonight, Mimi's voice on the phone; and about earlier in the day at school, Mimi raising her hand first. Did she know somehow that he liked her, too? Didn't girls know everything and just pretend not to? He felt guilty for liking her and looked away at the train. He was supposed to be helping his best friend. Tony should be there alone with Mimi. Tony trusted him. So why had Patrick come along? Why was he standing next to Tony's girlfriend wishing she liked him? Patrick decided to leave as soon as Tony came back.

"I have to go," Patrick told Mimi.

Without warning, Skip from Webster Groves High School walked up to them. He caught them by surprise as they faced the train. He was a handsome guy with the kind of long blond bangs girls love, blue eyes, and a blue jean jacket, bell bottoms, and waffle stomper boots. Patrick had seen him around the golf course and took a step back, wondering what was happening.

What's he doing here?

And then Mimi threw her arms around Skip's neck and hugged him.

Patrick looked around for Tony, but Tony was over in the honeysuckle peeing with his back to the excitement. Patrick noticed Skip's arms hanging limp at his sides. He didn't hug Mimi back. Then Skip took his hands and unpeeled Mimi from around his neck. Skip looked at Mimi's face. Patrick looked at Mimi's face, too. She looked like she was about to cry—like she'd already been crying. Coal cars rattled by. Mimi said something to Skip that Patrick couldn't hear.

"I'm sorry," he said slicing his hand sideways with finality, "but I'm breaking up with you. I've got a new girlfriend … at school."

Tony zipped up and struggled to refasten the enormous horsehead belt buckle, still unaware of what was happening.

"If you break up, I'll kill myself," Mimi blurted.

"Kill yourself?" Skip laughed. "Mimi, get real."

Patrick and Skip watched Mimi reach in her pocket and pull something out. They blinked, then stared.

It was a hand grenade—the realest looking hand grenade either one of them had ever seen. It wasn't plastic. It looked solid and deadly.

"I'll do it," she warned. A rusty boxcar passed by—*ka-klunk, ka-klunk, ka-klunk.*

"What the—?" Skip took a step back, mouth hanging open.

Mimi pulled the pin.

Skip and Patrick, like every boy, knew the facts of life, which were that when you pull the pin on a hand grenade, that's it. You only have a few seconds before it blows. Skip pawed the air trying to grab the grenade, but Mimi turned her back to him and stuffed it down her blouse.

Patrick and Skip looked at each other.

Time stood still.

Skip cussed and turned and ran home as fast as he could.

Patrick dove at Mimi, pushing her down, pinning her to the ground. He pushed her arms away, grabbed at her chest, and stuck his hand down her blouse.

"Get back, it's gonna blow!" she yelled, fighting him.

Arriving back on the scene, Tony stopped. "Hey, what's gives?"

"She's got a grenade!" Patrick yelled.

"Holy shit!" Tony belly-flopped on the grass ten feet away and covered his head. Patrick's hand groped around inside Mimi's blouse. He felt something strange and wonderful. This was it. He'd finally made it to second base. Now he was going to die.

But instead of dying, he kept groping until he finally found it. Mimi kept trying to stop him, but her hands were outside her blouse and his were inside. He grabbed the grenade, yanked his hand out of Mimi's shirt, scrambled to one knee, and threw it as fast and far as he could.

"Take cover!" Patrick yelled throwing himself on top of Mimi.

The grenade landed on the putting green and rolled to a stop six feet from the hole. They all three waited with their eyes shut tight. Nothing. The caboose rattled by and the train was gone. Patrick and Tony looked at each other. They looked at Mimi. She had fainted.

CHAPTER 12

THE LAST TIME Mimi fainted in a crisis was fifth grade. It was the night of the school championship spelling bee to determine who would go on to represent Mary Queen of Our Hearts in the regional rounds. The gymnasium was packed with parents and students. The stage was lit. Mimi was up there in a white dress with six other finalists. Sister Mathilda, who organized the event, was aglow in the podium light in her black habit and thick reading glasses, straining through cataracts to read the spelling words.

"Our next word goes to Mimi Maloney," Sister Mathilda said. "Are you ready?"

"Yes, Sister."

The crowd applauded. Mimi smiled.

"The word is 'meticulous'. How do you spell 'meticulous'?"

Mimi took a breath. It was not a word she knew. Meticulous, meticulous, meticulous. She sounded it out in her head. "I will now spell 'meticulous'," she began.

The crowd leaned forward.

"Meticulous... M-E-T-..." She stopped to be careful. It could be spelled 'metickulous' or 'mettickuluss' or 'metiqueluss' or maybe some other way. *Shit*.

"You have fifteen seconds," Sister Mathilda said gently.

Mimi's tongue pressed on the roof of her mouth.

"You have ten seconds."

The crowd shifted and murmured.

"Five seconds ..." Mimi's face got hot in the stage lights. Her throat tightened and she couldn't breathe. She blacked out.

When she opened her eyes on the gym floor, she was looking up at the faces of Sister Mathilda and the other contestants who were looking down on her. She wanted to lay there for ten thousand years and never move until everyone died and the stone school building blew away into dust.

"Get up," Sister Mathilda said. "We have to move on."

"I have to move on," Mimi said finally, sitting up on the fairway next to Tony and Patrick.

They both looked at her. She had been out for half a minute.

"What?" Patrick said.

"Take my hand," Tony said.

"I can get up on my own." She stood up and wiped the tears from her eyes and looked out at the hand grenade on the putting green and laughed.

"Are you okay?" Patrick said.

"You could've got killed," Tony said.

She shook her head and looked at Patrick. "Thanks. Thanks for helping. I'm sorry." She looked at Tony. "I'm sorry I brought you here."

"Who was that guy?" Tony asked.

"What was this all about?" Patrick said.

Mimi faced the facts front and center. "He was nobody. It was nothing. I gotta go. I gotta get that thing and put it back on the shelf. I've got homework." She started to walk toward the putting green, but the boys held her back.

"Whoa, wait a minute," Patrick said.

"Yeah, you can't go near that thing. It could blow at any minute! You pulled the pin."

"I got the pin," she said, holding it up. "I'll just put it back in."

The boys laughed and explained to her that with hand grenades, you can never put the pin back in. "Once you pull the pin, it's changed forever," Patrick said.

Mimi looked at Tony to see if that was true.

"I swear," Tony said, "that's a live grenade. It can never go back to the way it was."

Mimi sat down Indian-chief style to think. The boys sat down facing her. She buttoned up her blouse and zipped up her pink windbreaker and stretched out her arms with her hands resting on her knees. Everyone was quiet. Mimi's face turned serious. The boys drank in the sight of her hair and her moist lips and bright green eyes. After a minute she slapped her hands on her thighs. "Here's what we'll do," she announced.

CHAPTER 13

TONY WALKED out of the dark creek tunnel into the moonlight wearing a metal trash can around his torso. He had gone garage scavenging, as Mimi suggested, and found the things they needed. He found a trashcan with a rusted bottom that he kicked out. He found a World War II helmet to cover his head, a hockey goalie mask to cover his face, and goalie pads to protect his legs. In one hand, he held a metal trashcan lid like a knight's shield. In the other was a long pole from a swimming pool with a bug skimming net on the end. He walked clanking and creaking onto the green while Mimi and Patrick sat halfway up Suicide Hill watching.

"You look great," Patrick yelled.

"Wonderful," Mimi yelled.

Tony stopped about fifteen feet from the grenade and looked back at Mimi. He was only doing this to impress her, and because he felt jealous that Patrick had saved her life earlier. And, besides, Patrick had put his hand in her shirt! He couldn't wait to ask Patrick about that. Mimi waved at him and he marched on.

"Be careful," Patrick yelled.

Tony flexed his shoulder muscles and held the trash can shield up to protect his face from any flying shrapnel. "Hail Mary full of grace, the Lord is with thee," Tony prayed softly, "Blessed art thou among women, and blessed is the fruit of thy womb, Jesus. Holy Mary Mother of God, pray for us sinners now and at the hour of our death, Amen." It was the first time he had prayed since his dog Brando got sick. At the time he was praying for Brando to get well. Poor old Brando, Tony thought, he used to walk him on this same golf course, and now they could soon be together again.

"What are you waiting for?" Mimi yelled.

"This one's for Brando," Tony yelled.

"Who's that?" Mimi whispered to Patrick.

"That's his dog who died."

Peeking around the edge of the shield, Tony gently jabbed the pole forward, pushing the rim of the bug skimming net along the putting green toward the grenade like a dustpan. The net rim bumped the grenade. Tony winced and stopped. The grenade started to wobble.

"Lookout," Mimi yelled. The grenade was rolling down the slope of the green toward the cup.

"Don't' let it go in the hole. Move around it," Patrick yelled.

Tony shuffled and clanked to the left and slid the net in front of the cup. The grenade had enough momentum that it skipped over the rim into the net.

"You got it!" Patrick yelled.

Tony nodded and waved for them to be patient. This was the hard part. With eyes shut bracing for the explosion, he lifted the pole up off the green. The grenade started flopping and bouncing on the mesh fabric like a Webelo on a trampoline.

"Easy does it!" Mimi called out.

Now sweating heavily through his gold paisley disco shirt beneath his trash can armor, Tony steadied the pole and walked backwards through the valley of the shadow of death—the sand trap. Grunting for strength, and style, Tony hoisted the poll overhead and catapulted the grenade into the air toward the pond. Like raccoons on trash night, he dove into the sand trap with a crash. The grenade splashed into the pond with a quick, white whoosh. There was no explosion. Nothing. It sank to the leafy bottom four feet below and rested there.

"You did it," Patrick yelled.

Mimi ran down the hill to Tony. Standing up to kiss her, Tony reached out his arms, but the trashcan around his torso fell and he tumbled over again into the sand trap. Mimi sat down next to him and Patrick plopped down, too.

"Tony, great job," Mimi said.

"You were great," Patrick said.

"Thanks, it was a little hairy," Tony said removing the hockey mask. Mimi wiped the sweat off his forehead with her hand and looked at the pond.

"It's hot. Gonna be summer soon and all this will be behind us," Mimi said.

Tony wriggled out of the trashcan and got his bearing. He pulled out a pack of Camel non-filters and offered one to Mimi and Patrick. They both took one, and Tony got out his Zippo lighter and lit everyone's smoke. "Three on a match, it's bad luck," he said.

"I don't even smoke," Mimi said, puffing away.

"I was born with a Camel in my hands," Tony said.

"I'm quitting after this summer," Patrick said, "Some day my lungs will be pink and new again."

"High school," Mimi said sighing, "I was accepted to Holy Footsteps, but I don't know what I'll do." She was thinking about the fake letter she would have to intercept before her mom opened it.

"I guess you're worried about getting into high school with that snow globe shit," Tony said.

Patrick took a drag on his cigarette and looked at Tony. Tony was fluffing up his wavy black hair with his hand and flirting with a confession. "I guess you wonder who really did it," he said, "I mean, who do you think would have the balls to put that snow globe up there?"

"I don't know." Mimi looked at Tony and then at Patrick. Patrick looked at the sand to avoid her eyes. "I give up," she said.

Tony flicked his ashes and looked at Patrick. He back-slapped Patrick on the arm. Patrick narrowed his eyes at Tony to warn him to shut up. "Go, ahead," Tony said to Patrick, "Tell her. I trust her."

Mimi looked at Patrick, and he weakened. She did have the greenest eyes.

"Can you keep a secret?" he asked.

Mimi laughed. "Can *I* keep a secret? I was going to ask *you* the same thing. Can you keep a secret about all this tonight?"

The boys nodded in agreement.

"OK," she said. "Who did it?"

So, they talked and they smoked in the sand trap in the moonlight. Tony embellished the snow globe story to make it sound as if he had been plotting for months some way to get even with Miss Kleinschmidt, to teach her a lesson for her years of cruelty. He described how high and dangerous it was to put that snow globe in Mary's grip, and no one in the school knew the secret except Mimi, Tony said, because she was special.

"After we get caught," Patrick said, "Tony and me are leaving."

"Leaving?"

"Yeah, on a freight train." Patrick spoke in reverential tones about how the train tracks had been inviting him to run away from the future, how after eight years of grade school, he felt empty and trapped and didn't want to end up working downtown like all the dads. "Society is just moving us through these school buildings like holding pens, because society isn't ready for us yet," Patrick said. "Tony's coming with me."

Mimi looked at Tony to see if he was going to run away.

"Maybe," Tony said admiring Mimi's eyes.

Mimi laughed. "Don't worry about running away. You won't get caught. If you need some help, I mean, I can teach you how to lie. I'm so good at it I sometimes fool myself."

The boys looked at each other. Maybe Mimi could help. She did seem to have a way of handling things. "It's only two weeks until graduation, and then it's summer," she said. She grabbed two fistfuls of sand and threw them up in the air with the cigarette clamped in her grinning lips. They all three put their right hands together and swore to keep each other's secrets and gave a little team holler the way they did at CYC basketball games. Only this time, they were playing against the adults. Tony and Patrick were both in love with her now. But Mimi—she was her own girl.

CHAPTER 14

BEFORE SCHOOL the next morning, Archdiocese's special investigator Father Ernst along with Detective Kurtz convened a meeting with church and school officials to explain how the snow globe investigation would unfold. Miss Kleinschmidt and the school principal, Sister Helen—a nun in modern habit—were sitting at the table in the rectory basement next to an empty chair awaiting the arrival of the head priest of the parish, Monsignor O'Day.

"We can't let them get away with this," Miss Kleinschmidt said, sipping a cup of hot water with a bullion cube in it. Her breath smelled of chicken broth and cigarettes.

"With God's help, we will find the truth," said Father Ernst. He wore his usual black priest uniform, and his long leather coat rested over the back his chair. He was scanning a Vatican monthly newsletter article on recent sightings of Mary in South America.

"We have to be ready to be tough, to be assertive, and to use the most modern investigative techniques," added Detective Kurtz. Clad in a clean, blue uniform shirt he had ironed that morning, Kurtz drummed his fingernails on the wooden desk and looked at the clock. It was 7:35. Everyone, including Monsignor O'Day, was supposed to be there at 7:30.

"He said he would come," Sister Helen said. "He's probably just arranging some official papers for the meeting." More than anyone, Sister Helen was familiar with the late arrivals of Monsignor O'Day. She fidgeted with her short gray hair, which she had cut every few weeks to stay businesslike and efficient.

"Maybe he's not coming," Detective Kurtz said, "Maybe he's ill today. Let's get started."

The door from the priestly kitchen above the rectory creaked opened, and Monsignor O'Day, wearing black pants and a white shirt with his sleeves rolled up and top button undone, descended the steps with a plate of Eggo waffles, lightly humming "When Irish Eyes are Smiling".

Everyone stood to greet him. "Monsignor," they all said as he sat down.

"Oh, please sit down, forgive my late breakfast. I was reading the sports section after 6:30 Mass and forgot the time."

"Monsignor O'Day," Sister Helen said, "this is Father Ernst and Detective Kurtz. They're here to help with the investigation."

Monsignor O'Day nodded to them and picked up his fork. Detective Kurtz eyed the stack of three Eggo waffles with two pats of butter and maple syrup running down the side.

"We can't let whoever did this get away with it," said Miss Kleinschmidt. "I have some ideas who did it."

"Oh, I forgot my napkin," Monsignor O'Day said. "Never mind. I'll just be careful. My mother used to make me waffles when I was a lad. She was a loving person. Were you men close to your mothers?"

"Why, of course," Father Ernst said. "She was very devoted, to the church and to me. Her name was Mary."

Everyone looked over at Detective Kurtz. "My mother and I were very close when I was young, yes."

Monsignor O'Day cut a big section of waffle and lifted it halfway to his mouth. "I'm sorry, did she pass away?" O'Day said.

"No, she's still living."

O'Day nodded thoughtfully. "Well, what do you mean you 'were close when you were young'?" he said. "Are you still close?"

Everyone looked at Kurtz. This question was not on the agenda.

"In our own way, yes, but I don't mind saying ... well, I suppose she still holds a grudge about the speeding ticket I gave her when I was on motorcycle patrol."

"How fast was she going?"

"Thirty-five in a thirty."

"You gave your own mother a ticket for just going five miles over?"

"The law is blind."

O'Day pushed away his plate and pulled a deck of playing cards from his shirt pocket. Sister Helen rubbed her forehead, dreading a display of Queen of Hearts card tricks again. "Monsignor O'Day," Sister Helen said, "these men have volunteered their time to share with us their plans for the investigation."

"Probably just some boys blowing off steam, end of the year pranks," O'Day said. "Do you really think an investigation is the way to go? I mean have you been outside today? It's a lovely spring day. We need to open a window down here."

Father Ernst cleared his throat and sat up straight in his chair. "Monsignor O'Day, it is indeed a lovely spring day, and when I was chatting with the archbishop in the garden at the basilica before I came here, he expressed his full support for our efforts to root out this sin."

"That's right, it's a sacrilege," said Miss Kleinschmidt, getting a pack of Benson and Hedges 100s from her purse, "and whoever did it should not be allowed to breeze into some Catholic high school. You mind if I smoke?"

Monsignor O'Day nodded his permission and shuffled the deck of cards from hand to hand. "Did the archbishop really say all that stuff?"

"Yes, Monsignor," Father Ernst assured him.

"Let's look at this from a police standpoint," Detective Kurtz said. He pushed back his chair on the rectory floor, still sticky from trivia night beer spillage, and stood up. "This zip code has seen a wave of unsolved juvenile delinquency for years—kids opening fire hydrants, throwing tomatoes and peaches at buses, letting the air out of police tires, naked pool hopping."

"I used to go skinny dipping myself years ago," Monsignor O'Day said, smiling.

"We can't make light of this," Detective Kurtz continued. "If they get away with this crime against the church, what will they try to do in fifteen years when they're running the world? Steal from some company? Steal from the church? We have to send a message that the law is the law. And I think whoever stole this snow globe will be able to provide police with a wealth of information about all these other crimes that could one day blossom into something that could really threaten public safety. We have to teach them a lesson they'll never forget." Kurtz sat down. Everyone looked at Monsignor O'Day for his ruling.

"Okay, but tell me one thing. Does your mother still go thirty-five in a thirty?"

Monsignor O'Day thought he had him, but Detective Kurtz had an answer. "No, she lost her license. She hit a child and lost her license."

The table fell silent. This admission was news to everyone at the table, and it gave them all a sense of holy urgency for the investigation. Monsignor O'Day put away his playing cards and listened. Father Ernst and Detective Kurtz outlined their plans to interrogate each student from Miss Kleinschmidt's class individually. Before they could start, they requested a file on each student with their academic and disciplinary records for the year, along with photos of each child to examine for hints of rebellion. The investigation was now officially sanctioned and underway. Everyone shook hands with Monsignor O'Day and left him alone in the rectory basement. He sat back down to pick at his waffles and think about his mother.

CHAPTER 15

A SLOW FREIGHT MOANED AND CREAKED its way along the track, and Patrick ran up the embankment to have a look. It was a gentle train of big, rusty boxcars with wide open doors. The kind of train that wants to be hopped. But he had to go to school, so he stood in the middle of the two sets of tracks, about two feet from the train watching it. His spied a ladder with hand grips passing by and looked at a footrest where it would be so easy to land a shoe on the chipped paint and head off someplace else.

When he was younger, he and his friends would catch a freight train down into the business district to go to the Ben Franklin or the Velvet Freeze. But everyone had good bikes now and they had all cast train hopping aside as immature. All but Patrick. He still had thoughts about it, mostly at night. Or in the day, when he walked to school. Or when he walked home from school along the tracks.

Lying in bed, he'd hear a passing freight and think about his unmet calling. The tracks knew what he wanted. The tracks knew that if he ever got really bored, or in bad trouble, he could go there and grab a boxcar and see where it might take him. His only problem was that he had no real troubles to run away from. Unfortunately, his parents loved him. And his brothers and sisters were good to him. He shared a room with his older brother John, who was a freshman at St. Aloysius. So he had that to look forward to, going to high school with his brother. But even so, the tracks knew what he really wanted and they were always there, waiting for him to give in. Waiting for him to join them.

A speeding freight train on the second set of tracks sounded its horn.

Shit. Patrick flinched and turned. It was charging toward him a hundred feet up the line by the golf course. He stood still in the no man's zone between the twin sets of tracks. The engineer laid on the horn ordering him to get off the tracks. Now. Move fast. Run for your life!

Patrick gave him a gentle wave of the hand. The engineer was furious. The front of the engine shot toward his spot, its horn blaring one long, solid *Holy Shit* note that bent into a lower key as it shot passed him. Now he was between two trains going in opposite directions. He looked up. Blue sky above—rushing, grinding metal on either side. His hair whipped up and twisted in the whirlwind. Wheels as sharp as butcher knives sliced and thumped all around him. His thin blue uniform tie pulled to one side in the vacuum of wind sucking under the cars of the fast train. Dust and grit picked at his face, and he squinted against it. If he wanted, he could reach out his arms and touch both trains. But he kept them clamped tight at his sides and listened to the metallic melody. The trains hummed and groaned and roared like the shout of all the dead wishing they were living again, and only Patrick was alive in the middle to hear it.

And then it stopped.

The trains passed. Dust settled. Quiet returned. And standing there looking at him by the side of the black bridge was Tony and Mimi.

"What the hell?" Tony said.

Patrick looked at Tony to see if he felt the same way about the trains. But he didn't. The only thing he was feeling was being with Mimi.

Mimi walked over in the middle of the tracks, looking both ways to be safe, and Tony followed. "I've got a plan," she said.

"She told me some of it," Tony said, "but the rest she wanted to wait for you. We were looking for you."

"Did your dad notice the grenade missing?" Patrick asked her.

Mimi rubbed her nose a little worried, but not too much. "No, not yet, probably tonight he'll notice."

"What are you gonna say?" Patrick asked.

She shrugged. "I don't know. Probably just say I don't know what happened. We did have a party last night, so anybody could have borrowed it. I'm not worried about that." She took a breath, worried about something else.

"What?" Tony said.

"Tony, I need you and Patrick to steal a letter from the mailman today at my house."

Patrick and Tony looked at each other.

"No way," Patrick said. "Are you kidding?"

She turned to Patrick and put her hand on his shoulder like Joan of Arc assigning a soldier an important battle task. "It will help me with the snow globe investigation to get this one thing out of the way."

Tony saw her hand on Patrick's shoulder and grabbed her other hand. "What do you want us to do?"

She laid out her plan, glancing back and forth at them. It was a daring idea that would mean sneaking away from the playground at recess and getting back just in time for the next class. Mimi told them for the first time that she had sneaked into Holy Footsteps Academy a while back to get some letterhead and that she had mailed the fake letter rescinding her acceptance to the school. Patrick and Tony traded glances. They didn't tell her they had followed her that day.

Mimi was also holding back something. What she didn't tell them was she also had a second piece of school letterhead and an envelope, one she had taken in case of a typing mistake. Instead, she used it last night, after she came home from the golf course, to type another fake letter from the school saying they were looking forward to her coming and wished her a safe summer. That letter she could maybe swap out with the first letter when it arrived—if Patrick and Tony failed in their mission.

"We can't just walk up to a mailman and rob him," Patrick said. "He'll see us and tell the police what we look like."

Tony kept quiet, because that was true.

"Here's my plan," Mimi said. She opened up her book bag and pulled out two pair of aqua blue dishwashing gloves.

"What's that for?" Tony said.

"Can't leave fingerprints," Mimi said. Then she got out two facemasks. One was a black wool ski mask and the other was a rubber Halloween mask of President Nixon. "Just put these on, run and grab the letter, and no one will know who you are."

"That'll never work. He'll still see our ties and uniforms and know it's somebody from the school," Patrick said.

Tony twisted his tie.

"I thought of that. You'll just have to strip down to your underwear."

The boys looked at each other and burst out laughing.

"No way in hell. Someone will see us," Patrick said.

"Don't worry. I've been in my underwear outside before and nobody saw me."

Patrick and Tony tried not to glance at each other as Mimi kept talking. They both studied her eyes and her hair and her lips and thought of her pale skin and white underwear gleaming in the bright after-school sun. The train tracks stretched out behind her onto the bridge deck and down the long straight away that ran along the golf course. The scrub brush that grew along the sides of the track was mint green and budding. How could they say no to her, a girl standing there like a wildflower, asking them, essentially, if they were brave enough to do this one little thing for her?

"I'll do it," Tony said, "as long as I can wear the ski mask."

Patrick looked at the Nixon mask and then at Mimi's green eyes.

"I've got a whole plan for the snow globe investigation," she said, "but first we just need to get this letter out of the way."

They agreed to rob the mailman in front of her house during recess, and then they walked to school, arriving as Father Ernst and Detective Kurtz entered the school building to examine the student files in the office.

"Class," Miss Kleinschmidt said, "We're going to rehearse your graduation ceremony in the gym today, after recess. But first, today in history ..."

The morning hours passed slower than picking an elbow scab that wasn't ready to come off yet. Miss Kleinschmidt opened the windows that faced the school's front lawn and the rows of big houses across the street. Fresh air and birdsong, and the purr of passing traffic reminded the students there was an outside world they would soon be a part of, a free world beyond eighth grade. But they had to get through the next two weeks and the snow globe investigation and another long morning of captivity. First there was algebra, and social studies, and reading time. Patrick got out his book on Dillinger and read the part where Dillinger knocked off a bank in Greencastle, Indiana. It was a corner bank across from the town courthouse along a row of busy shops.

Dillinger and the gang stepped out of the sunshine into the bank with guns drawn announcing a holdup. The teller on duty, a nervous young man, led them to the safe. It was a double combination safe, and the teller had to dial the numbers just right or it wouldn't open. He got it open and later told the newspaper, "It was easy with a Tommy gun pointed at my head." Dillinger and the gang made off with $70,000 in cash and securities without firing a shot. It was Dillinger's biggest haul. Afterwards, they hid out at a lake house in the area while police everywhere were looking for them. But they couldn't find Dillinger. He was too smart.

At recess, Patrick and Tony drifted over near the fence, and looked around. Sister Mathilda, the blind nun in the black habit, was going back and forth on the dog-run line. A couple of Mothers' Club guards were over by some first graders commenting on how big the girls were getting and how soon they'd be eighth graders. "If only they could stay this way," the Mothers' Club guard said. That's when Mimi gave the boys a wink, and the two of them slipped through the break in the fence into the backyards that ran behind the playground. Racing along, jumping hedges, and weaving around birdbaths, they rounded the corner at the far end of the playground and cut through a yard beside the priests' house. Father Maligan, the ancient priest who was practically deaf, smoked his pipe and read the horse racing section of the sports page by his open window. He didn't see them. No one did.

They stripped down to their underwear in some bushes at the house next door to Mimi's. Tony grabbed the ski mask and held it ready. Patrick picked up the Nixon mask and looked at the nose.

"Why are we doing all this?" Patrick asked.

"Hell if I know. We better put on the gloves."

They put on the rubber gloves and watched for the mailman, reviewing their plans for the heist.

"When he gets here—if he gets here—we'll wait until his back is turned as he goes up the hill to Mimi's house."

"I know," Tony said.

"Then we'll run out and grab his bag."

"I know."

"And we'll keep running two more yards that way, then hang a right and loop back here through the back yards to get our clothes."

"Patrick?"

"Yeah?"

"What was it like?"

"What?"

"When you got the grenade?"

"You saw. I just grabbed it and threw it right away and ducked."

"No, I mean when you put your hand in her shirt looking for it, what was that like?"

Patrick didn't want to talk about that again. Tony had already asked him about eight times. He stretched out his hands and looked at his fingers in the aqua blue rubber gloves. "It was nothing. It was just real quick."

"Come one, I gotta know. Can you describe them?"

"What?"

"Don't give me that shit. You know what I'm talking about."

"It all happened so fast."

"Come on, I have to know because you know I like Mimi. I'm just afraid that after what happened. You might like her, too. Maybe she even likes you better than me."

Patrick put on the Nixon mask and looked at Tony. "Look, I'm telling you the truth. She doesn't like me, and I don't like her. I swear. You saw her first. You're the one for her. Not me. I'm just a helper. I mean, you saw her first, remember?"

"That's right," Tony said smiling. He started boogie dancing in his underwear to limber up. He was feeling better.

Patrick felt his hot, lying breath steaming up inside the Nixon mask. How could he be such a cheat to his best friend? Tony's heart was set on Mimi, so Patrick decided—again—to try to not like her anymore, to only see the bad things about her and find fault with her. But he couldn't think of any. Mimi had all the essential qualities a girl needed—beauty, intelligence, and she was always in trouble.

"Here he comes," Tony whispered putting on his ski mask.

The mailman approached the yard unaware he was being watched. He was a portly man in his forties, fond of fishing, and daydreaming about the upcoming Memorial Day weekend at Bull Shoals Lake and Resort that was just two weeks away. On last year's trip, he got a sudden violent jerk on his line from a fish that awoke him from a nap in his shore chair. The drag on his reel was whining and grinding as the fish pulled out more and more line. He leaped up, planted his feet in the mud and gripped the pole as tight as he could, fighting with the unseen fish for two minutes before it shot up above the water. It was a large mouth bass, a five pounder.

Patrick and Tony ran up behind the mailman.

The fish arced and skipped and thrashed and buffeted across the sun streaked lake chop. "You're not getting away from me," the mailman told the fish.

Just then the mailman felt a violent tug on his leather bag shoulder strap. It slipped off his shoulder and fell halfway down his arm. But he cocked his elbow shut tight, pinning the strap between his arm muscles, and looked to see what it was.

Two boys in nothing but white underwear and masks were yanking on the mailbag.

The mailman's heart hammered. "I've got you," he yelled. The boys jerked and twisted and pulled on the strap. Swatting them with a fistful of letters in his left hand, the mailman kept his bag strap tight in his clenched right arm. He danced toward the boys on the sloped lawn, letting them run with the bait a little to tire them out. They fought and pulled, moving about eight feet away from the spot of the original strike. It was no use. Patrick and Tony were panting inside their masks, losing energy. Their naked skin was pink with over exertion. "You're not getting away from me," the mailman thundered. But just as he said that—the strap went slack.

Tony gave it one more sudden pull and the mailbag snapped loose from the shoulder strap. The mailman fell backwards one way, and the boys fell backwards the other.

"Let's go," Tony yelled.

The boys jumped up and Patrick took the mailbag. They ran through front yards barefoot in the grass while the mailman watched lying on his back. Patrick started throwing out a trail of coupons and junk mail, bank statements and anything that didn't look like a regular letter Mimi had described. They darted to the right between two houses and started looping back to get their clothes.

"Have you got it?" Tony said running.

"I'm looking for the last name," Patrick said tossing out more utility bills and credit card offers addressed to Mimi's neighbors. They passed a retired man in one back yard practicing his nine iron shots with a plastic golf ball. He wore a light windbreaker and was whistling "Stardust." His back was to them and he didn't see a thing.

The mailman clambered to his feet and tucked in his shirt. He picked up some letters he had dropped and stumbled up the front steps of Mimi's house and pounded on the door. Mimi's mother, who had been on the sofa watching *The Young and the Restless*, jumped up to unlock the door.

"What's wrong?"

The mailman leaned against the doorframe, panting. "Call the police. They attacked me."

"Who?" She looked around.

"Nixon and another guy, both in their underwear."

Mimi's mom leaned farther out the front door and saw the trail of letters on the lawns. The mailman handed her a stack of bills—and Mimi's letter—which had been in his delivery hand when the attack began.

Patrick and Tony reached the bushes where their clothes were hidden and fell to their knees. They took off their masks. Patrick dumped over the mailbag in the mud. They rifled through the letters with their gloved hands.

"I can't find it. There's nothing here."

"Well, we can at least tell her the good news. There was no mail for her house today."

Mimi's mom threw the mail down atop the closed lid of the upright piano and called the police. She brought the mailman a glass of water, which he drank sitting on the front porch steps. He was getting his breath back and told her a little about the holdup. "Same thing happened to me at Bull Shoals," he said. "You have to keep the line tight, or it might break."

Patrick and Tony got dressed, ran back to the bridge, ditched the masks and gloves there, and sped through yards like Dillinger after a bank heist to get back before recess was over. When they arrived in the gap of the back playground fence, their classmates were lining up to go up the gym steps for graduation rehearsal. They ran up last in line, wiped sweat from their faces with their uniform ties, and climbed the steps into the gymnasium.

"What do you think Mimi will say?" Tony whispered.

"I don't know, but whatever she says, I'm not going back again tomorrow."

CHAPTER 16

THAT NIGHT AT DINNER, Mimi sat in her place next to her dad. She was wearing shorts with knee high socks, and the second fake letter from Holy Footsteps Academy—the letter saying they were looking forward to her coming—was tucked neatly out of view inside her right sock. It was licked shut inside a stamped official school envelope addressed to her parents. To make the postage stamp look canceled, Mimi had drawn squiggly lines across it with a blue ink pen.

Mimi's mind was racing, because her mother had told her about the mailman being robbed—but somehow their mail got through. Somewhere in the house that first fake letter was lying around. Mimi knew her mom hadn't read it or she would have said something. So Mimi had scoured the first floor looking for it—under the couch pillows, in the desk, on the mantle, in the den—but couldn't find it. Now she and her dad were at the dinner table alone waiting for everyone else. Mimi's sister was playing scales, up and down, on and on. The only good thing was no one had noticed the missing hand grenade.

"Mimi, have you seen the mail?" her dad asked.

"Why, no. I haven't. Have you?"

"No, but I'm expecting an important letter from the office and your mother just told me there was some kind of hooliganism with the mailman."

"Time for dinner," Mimi's mom called as she emerged from the kitchen.

She was holding a supper dish and stood at the end of the dining room table. "Come on, guys, time for dinner."

Mimi heard her brother switch off the TV, and her sister stop playing scales. But Mimi didn't see her sister put away her scale book and close the lid on the piano because if she had, she'd have known exactly where the missing mail was. When Mimi's sister had come home from school, she'd flipped up the piano lid to practice, obscuring the mail from view. Now that she'd stopped for dinner, the mail that had been hidden from view flopped into sight and the letter from Holy Footsteps Academy fell on the rug. She picked it up and tossed it back on the piano with the rest of the mail.

Mimi's sister and brother came in and they all sat down. "Hurry up, let's eat," Mimi's dad said. "Smells like your mother's made a us another wonderful dinner." He looked across the table at her with respect. "I don't know how you do it."

"Oh, it's nothing," she said with a smile.

"It's not nothing, darling. It's like you run your own successful corporation right here."

Mimi's mom blushed at the compliment and set down the apricot chicken casserole with white rice. For sides, there were green beans and fresh baked crescent rolls. It was quiet, like a golf tournament, as Mimi's mom looked at her dad to signal him to say grace.

"In the name of the Father and the Son and the Holy Ghost," he said. Everyone made the sign of the cross while looking down at their plates bright with dishwasher shine. "Bless us oh Lord and these thy gifts which we are about to receive from thy bounty through Christ our Lord, Amen."

The whole family said the "amen" part together, then did the sign of the cross again and looked up at the food. Mimi wasn't hungry. She had eaten three Twinkies during the failed letter search and had downed a big glass of milk to calm her nerves.

"Now, what's all this about the mailman?" Mimi's dad said, serving himself some apricot chicken and rice. He passed it to Mimi, who wrinkled her nose and took just a little bit.

"I told you, he was robbed," Mimi's mom said from her end of the table.

"I never heard of such a thing."

"Did they have guns, Mom?" Mimi's little brother asked.

"No, the mailman said they were boys in underwear and masks."

Everyone laughed. Mimi noticed she wasn't laughing, so she worked up a fake one to blend in.

"We shouldn't laugh," Mimi's mom said, scolding herself. "The mailman was quite upset. I can't understand why this would happen on our front lawn."

"Probably a coincidence," Mimi said. "Please, pass the rolls."

"I'm expecting an important piece of mail from work," Mimi's dad said chewing away on string beans.

"Don't worry, our mail got through," Mimi's mom said, "I just can't remember where I put it in all the excitement."

Mimi's sister slugged back some milk and put down her glass with a gasp and a thump. "It's on the piano. I just saw it."

"I'll get it for you," Mimi said, shooting out of her chair.

"Mimi, sit down," her mom said before Mimi had a chance to get to the living room. "You haven't touched your dinner. Look at your sister's plate. She knows how to eat. I'll get the mail."

Mimi sat back down and pushed around her chicken and rice with her fork. She sensed her dad eyeing her, so she put some in her mouth and started chewing.

"Here it is," Mimi's mom said, sitting back down. "Let's see, bills, bills, bills, I don't see anything from your work, dear."

Mimi's dad put down his fork. "Let me see … please pass me the mail."

The mail crossed the table from Mimi's mom to Mimi's sister and then to Mimi. Before she handed it to her dad, she could see the edge of the first fake letter from Holy Footsteps—the one saying they had no room for her—sticking out from the bottom of the stack.

"Thank you, Mimi," her dad said, taking the letters. He breathed through his nose and the table was quiet as he rifled through the mail. "That's what's wrong with the mail," he said. "A man works all day downtown, expecting some bit of good news to arrive, maybe a letter from an old friend, and there's nothing here but intrusions into my wallet."

"What letter are you looking for?" Mimi's brother asked.

"It's my parking decal to go with my promotion. It's just a little orange sticker, but it represents years of hard work. It means I can park in the front row with the other executives near the door instead of having to hunt all over the parking lot on cold, snowy days trying to find a spot with hundreds of other people."

"Are you the Number One guy now?" Mimi's brother asked.

"No, not the Number One guy, but one of the top guys." He shook his head and looked at the mail. "You wouldn't know it from all this blood sucking mail besieging me. Look at this." He started to open some bills.

"Honey, let's not open any bills at dinner," Mimi's mom said. "It's unsettling."

"All right, no bills, but let me see, let me show you what other kind of bothersome mail descends upon a man after he's fought downtown all day to come home for some peace with his family. What's this, now?"

Mimi held her breath. Her dad was opening another letter, not hers, some kind of letter with a lot of typing on it. She watched her dad's lips move as he read it, and she glanced down at the letter from Holy Footsteps, which was next on the stack. Mimi reached her hand toward the Holy Footsteps letter to flick it on the floor, where she could bend over to pick it up and make the switch.

"Listen to this outrage!" her dad said slapping his hand down on the Holy Footsteps envelope. Mimi's yanked her hand back. "Why this is a chain letter of the rankest kind, using religion to try to get into my wallet."

"What is it, Dad?" Mimi's sister asked.

"It's a pyramid scheme with the Hail Mary thrown in to fools us. They want me to send a dollar to ten people who got this letter before me, and then have me send copies of the letter to as many people as I can. That way, everyone below me will supposedly send me money later." He let out a "Hmmmph" with contempt and read on to himself.

"How much money can we get?" Mimi's brother asked.

"It says here, one man in Mexico City who obeyed the letter became a millionaire, and another man who broke the chain died suddenly. Can you believe this—"

"Are you gonna do it?" Mimi's brother asked.

"Of course not. These pyramid schemes only benefit the persons at the top and take advantage of the people below."

"Aren't you afraid of dying if you don't send it?" Mimi's sister said.

Mimi's mom cleared her throat. "Honey, God isn't going to let your father die, he just got a promotion. It wouldn't make sense."

"That's right," Mimi's dad said.

"Dad?"

"Yes, son?"

"Is your job a pyramid scheme? I mean with you and the other guys at the top and everyone below you?"

Mimi's dad let out a long, exasperated sigh. "Let's see what else we have here, a letter from Holy Footsteps. Probably another appeal for money to fix the roof or some new gym floor they dreamed up."

Mimi grabbed the letter in her dad's grip.

"Maybe I should open this," she said.

"Mimi!" her dad said holding the letter tight. He looked at her face. She was breathing heavily. "What's wrong with you?"

"Maybe it's for me. Maybe it's about how they're getting ready for me to go there next year. I heard some of the kids are getting those letters."

"Mimi, you act as if this letter were a bomb about to explode. Please let go."

She let go and lowered her head. Everyone looked at her. Her dad tore the leading edge of the letter and ripped his index finger across the top. "We'll see what new scheme those nuns are up to now."

"Dad," Mimi's brother said chewing a roll. "I forgot to tell you. When I was in the den I noticed that your hand grenade is gone."

Mimi's dad froze and looked up. "What did you say?"

"I just thought of it now when you said the word explosion. I was watching TV in the den and looked at the shelf. Your hand grenade isn't there."

Mimi's dad put down the letter from Holy Footsteps Academy on the table and leaped from his chair. He ran into the den with everyone following—everyone except Mimi. She stole the opened letter off the table and stuck it in her left sock, then pulled out the other fake letter from her right sock, ripped open the envelope and put it on the table. With no one looking, she put the rest of her dinner on her sister's plate and got up and danced around the dining room table swinging her arms with joy. Then she wiped the smile off her face with her hands and whisked into the den to look concerned about the missing grenade.

CHAPTER 17

PRESIDENT NIXON stripped naked and put on his favorite U.S. Navy swimming trunks. He walked out of the changing room and headed toward the White House pool on super secret sublevel five, right down the hall from the continuity of government conference room and the Pepsi machine. He lowered himself to the edge and pulled on his fins, snapped his goggles into place, and slipped into the water.

It was peaceful and quiet under water, and he glided smoothly toward the other end—until he noticed something shiny down by the drain. What's that? he wondered. He kicked his legs, the fins thrusting him deeper and deeper. The President's ears popped and his lungs were tight, but on he swam down, down, down. Looks like a Lincoln penny. Honest Abe, my ass. If I can just get that penny, he told himself, this whole Watergate thing will blow over. All I have to do is reach that damn penny. He reached out his fingers to pluck it from the bottom when suddenly a dozen other pennies fell through the water and settled near the drain. Nixon looked up and saw a black figure looming at the end of the pool. He could no longer tell which was the original penny. A surge of bubbles came from his mouth as he cursed underwater. He kicked off the drain, shooting up to the surface.

Kissinger stood on the ledge empting his pockets into the water to get the President's attention. "Mr. President," Kissinger said as Nixon surfaced. "We have to talk. The live televised Senate Watergate Hearings begin today."

Nixon swam backstroke laps while Kissinger walked along poolside discussing the crisis.

"As you know, McCord will testify. He might paint a picture of presidential impropriety."

"Presidential impropriety? Bah," Nixon said kicking off the wall and reversing coarse. "I'll just tell them ... I'll tell them the truth."

Kissinger turned around to keep pace with the President. "How do you plan to phrase that? I mean, what is the truth, at this point, sir?"

Nixon kicked harder as his mind struggled to phrase the truth. Kissinger's pace quickened. His black wingtip shoes were getting wet, the chlorine water dulling their shine. "I'll just tell them ... I had no prior knowledge of the Watergate operation. I took no part in, nor was I aware of, any subsequent efforts that may have been made to cover up the damned thing."

"We should write that down, but do you think the American people will believe you?"

Nixon stopped and floated face down like a dead man. Kissinger waited. Nixon wasn't moving. Kissinger stared at the President's pale, white back. "Mr. President? Sir, are you all right?" Fearing a stroke, Kissinger dove in the pool in his suit and tie and swam over to rescue the President. Nixon saw him coming and treaded water, grinning.

"Good job, Henry. I was just testing you."

"Mr. President," Kissinger said, struggling to stay afloat, his suit coat billowing out around him, "how can you hope to hold it all together?"

"You know, Henry, in the service, when I was on Bouganville Island, I won a thousand dollars playing poker. You wanna know how I did it?"

Kissinger's heavy shoes and wet clothes were pulling him down. "How sir?"

"The Nixon poker face. See for yourself." The President fixed his face muscles to look like Rushmore, like a postage stamp of presidential credibility. "It works every time. Don't worry. Why don't you come by this afternoon and we'll watch it on TV together. Maybe Pat'll make some ginger snaps."

"I'm sorry, Mr. President, I'm playing tennis this afternoon with someone special," Kissinger said, water up to his chin.

"Someone special? What, some show girl or model?"

"She may have done some modeling at one time. I'm still gathering all the facts."

"Well, that's what you're good at, Henry. Don't worry about this Watergate thing. Just gather the facts, keep a poker face, and move forward. That's what I'm doing."

"Yes, sir, Mr. President." Kissinger swam over to the ladder and climbed out dripping wet and winded.

The President pulled his diving goggles over his eyes and dove back to the bottom in search of the lucky Lincoln penny that would solve everything.

CHAPTER 18

PATRICK AND TONY climbed the embankment up to the train bridge on the way to school. Mimi was already there waiting for them in her green plaid uniform skirt and white blouse. It was a cloudy day and rain threatened. It was the first day of the snow globe investigation and the authorities would start questioning students one by one. Mimi had said she had a plan, and the boys were keen to hear all about it.

"How'd everything go last night, I mean with the letter?" Tony said.

"Oh, fine."

"What about the grenade?" Patrick said.

"Well, Dad thinks maybe one of the junior executives who were in the den took it because they were jealous of his promotion."

"What does your mom think?" Tony asked.

"She never liked it anyway. She's just glad it's out of the house. Now, about this snow globe case, I've decided to go with the old pyramid scheme."

"Pyramid scheme?" Tony said.

Mimi had only heard about pyramid schemes the night before, but it taught her that she needed a system of telling all the students in the class what to say to the investigators without having them know where the instructions came from.

"I'll be at the top," Mimi said, "I'm Number One."

"Can I be Number Two?" Tony said.

Mimi turned toward him as Tony flexed his romantic eyebrows. "Sure, why not. And Patrick you can be Number Three."

"Fine, but what's your plan?"

The plan was for Number Two to tell a pair of students one theory of how the snow globe got up there, while Number Three would tell two students another theory of how it got up there. Everything had to be spoken. No passing notes. Those four students would be instructed to each tell another pair the theories that they heard, with instructions to pass them along down the pyramid. A student passing along his theory would ask another, "Have you been told yet what to say?" If the kid said "yes," the teller would find another student to tell, but if he said, "no," he'd tell him the theory he was supposed to pass on. Eventually every kid in the class would have instructions on what to say when questioned. No one was to tell the next person below who the next person above was. That way no one could trace back it all back to Number One.

"What's the point of all this?" Patrick asked.

"Yeah, why not just have everybody say the same thing?" Tony said.

"The point is to make it look natural like there are these different theories. One is that Miss Kleinschmidt might have done it."

"Hah! That's crazy. Why should they think she did it?"

"They both won't, but we'll do some things to make the detective think so, to let him think that she's crazy, and then with the other theory we'll get the priest to want to believe that one."

"What's the other theory?" Tony said.

"That it was a miracle," Mimi said.

"A miracle? You mean that somehow that snow globe just floated up there into Mary's hand? He won't fall for that," Patrick said.

"He doesn't have to. He just has to wonder why so many kids think it might have been a miracle. You heard him talk about that Mary stuff. It's divide and conquer. He'll eat it up. One more thing—"

"What?" Patrick said.

"I need each of you to give a different answer when they ask you who did it."

"What should we say?" Tony asked.

"I'll leave that up to you. Just both make up something different. That way everyone won't be saying the same thing. It'll sound more believable."

The plan seemed solid and one that would divide and conquer the investigators, so they agreed that Mimi was Number One—the top of the pyramid—and no one could know who Number One was. They walked down the embankment off the tracks and cut through yards to school. The gold statue of Mary on the church roof rose above the treetops against gray, black clouds thundering in the distance.

CHAPTER 19

MISS KLEINSCHMIDT STOOD BY HER DESK as fat drops of rain pounded the Mary Queen of Our Hearts parking lot outside. She wore a gray pants suit, heavy rouge on her cheeks, and a shade of lipstick that looked like burnt ox blood. "Today in history," she checked her notes, "May 17, 1849. A fire almost burns St. Louis to the ground." That seemed to satisfy her, some. She strutted about, rattling off her usual directives—don't slouch, listen up, write legibly—but she also radiated morbid anticipation, a hunger for the savory broth of judgment that was about to be served up hot. Professional investigators would soon be grilling her students to find out who stole the snow globe. This was going to be a good day. She had combed her wiry gray hair more than usual for the occasion, but it still loomed over the class like a volcanic plume over a mountain village.

"I hope everyone has had time to think hard about any sins that might be on your conscience," she said, "because the questioning is about to begin." She picked up a piece of paper from her desk. "I have in my hand a list of the students the investigators want to see." She glanced at it and looked up. "Up first is Mimi Maloney."

A crack of thunder rattled the windows as Mimi got up. Miss Kleinschmidt told her where to go, and the class watched as Mimi walked slowly toward the door, eyes forward, with no sign of emotion. She pulled open the door, went out in the hall, and pushed it closed behind her. The bolt clicked into the door jam, and every student looked up at Miss Kleinschmidt.

"This shouldn't take long, as long as the guilty ones admit what they've done." Then she repeated one of her favorite complaints. "It's just a shame that a few have to ruin it for everyone." Patrick and Tony's lips moved to her last words, which they had heard practically every day since September.

"After Mimi is done, numbers two and three will be questioned next," she said looking at the list. "Tony Vivamano and Patrick Cantwell." And with that a crack of lightning lit up the gloom outside followed by another low roll of window-rattling thunder.

Mimi knocked on the door of the interrogation room and waited. This was the same room where the school nurse had conducted eye exams in past years, the same room where Mimi had been taken to rest on the little cushioned bench after she had fainted during the fifth grade spelling bee. The door opened about six inches and the bulging, brown eyes of Father Ernst peered out at Mimi.

"Miss Maloney?"

"Yes?"

Father Ernst swung the door open wide. It was a recluse spider of a room, without windows and just one lamp on the nurse's desk. Detective Kurtz sat behind the desk. He rose without smiling to greet Mimi.

"Miss Maloney, won't you please sit down?" Detective Kurtz said. His tone was like a dentist about to do major drilling.

"Thank you," she said. She sat in a straight-back wooden chair facing the desk, crossed her legs, and straightened her skirt. She looked around the room to get her bearings. Father Ernst sat down on the red leather cushion bench off to the left. On the wall above him was a poster of the human anatomy showing a naked man with a cutaway view of his tendons and organs. The only other thing on the walls was the eye chart behind the desk. Detective Kurtz grabbed the metal coil neck of the desk lamp and twisted it to cast a harsh light in Mimi's face. Then he sat down and stared into her eyes

"How are you feeling just now?" he began.

"Special."

"Special?" Kurtz's eyes widened.

Mimi knew right away "special" had been the wrong word to start with. It sprung to her lips from her satisfaction with how well things had been going since being dumped on the golf course. Patrick had saved her from having her guts blown out by the hand grenade, and she had successfully switched the fake letters, fooling her whole family. Neither her older sister nor her younger brother could have done half so well. Not only that, Tony liked her and he and Patrick had both crowned her Number One at the top of the pyramid. For once, she was in charge of something big and even more elaborate than a Chopin piano piece or a basketball game. She was on a winning streak that put her beyond the reach of the detective or the priest. Her main problem—right this very instant—was not concealing any nervousness. She felt none. Instead she had to conceal her confidence. To her way of thinking, it was the Father Ernst and Detective Kurtz who should feel nervous. After all, they were just ordinary adults. They didn't know what kind of girl they were dealing with.

"Oh maybe that's the wrong word. Maybe I should say 'honored'. Yes, I feel honored that you called on me first, as if I'm anybody."

"Tell us about yourself," Father Ernst said folding his hands in a prayerful pose.

"Me? Oh, there's not much to tell. I'm just an average girl."

"Have you got a boyfriend?" Father Ernst asked.

"No, not me. I'm too young for all that. Besides, I've got too much homework. I want to keep my grades up because I'm going to Holy Footsteps next year."

"Why did you raise your hand?" Detective Kurtz said suddenly. "You were the first one to raise your hand when we asked who took the snow globe."

Mimi tipped her head left and right to look flighty and shallow. "I don't know. I've been asking myself the same question. Why? Why? Why? Whew, I guess, I just … wanted to see what the reaction would be. I get bored sometimes."

"Bored?" Father Ernst asked. He swallowed with a dry mouth out of empathy for the nervousness he supposed Mimi was feeling.

"Yes, that's a fault of mine. I get bored. Eighth grade just doesn't seem to matter." She sighed and held her face bored, wondering how to come up with a good explanation for her fake boredom.

"Please, tell us why you're bored," Father Ernst said. "We want to understand what you're thinking."

"Well, it's hard to say." Mimi had nothing to share. But then she remembered something Patrick said on the golf course and threw that in to sound deep. "I've been thinking. It's like we're all being held up in a pen, a big stone building of a pen with different rooms, and they're moving the kids through slowly, one year at a time. Society isn't ready for eighth graders yet, so they keep us in waiting and we've been at this school for eight years, really nine years, if you count the kindergarten house out back. It can get awfully dull. So along comes this mystery about the missing snow globe, and I guess I just got so bored I raised my hand looking for some excitement."

"Are you excited to be here now?" Detective Kurtz asked. Mimi could tell by the way he asked that he thought she was lying, and that was okay.

"Not really," she shrugged uncrossing her legs and swinging them off the edge of the chair. "I mean this is better than history, which I'm missing, but it's not as exciting as if I really did take the snow globe. Then you could solve the crime and maybe I'd be arrested and get on the news. But nothing that good ever happens to me. I'm just an average girl, I guess."

Father Ernst got off the bench and leaned over to whisper something to Detective Kurtz. Kurtz nodded. Then Ernst whooshed back down on the leather bench and started his own line of probing.

"What are your views on Mary?"

"On who?"

"The Blessed Mother. Surely you have some view on her after nine years at Mary Queen of Our Hearts."

Mimi stopped to think. She knew she should probably say she was big on Mary and really admired her, because that would support the lie she was about to tell about how the snow globe got into Mary's hand. "Well, when I think of Mary, I think of that one miracle with the wine."

"The wedding at Canaan? Jesus' first miracle," Father Ernst said.

"Was that his first? There's so many, I forget. But for me, I think of how Mary told Jesus to do something and he did it. That shows she has a lot of pull. She probably still does. Up there in heaven, if Mary gets bored and gets an idea for a miracle, she probably walks over to Jesus and tells him she needs a favor. If she wanted to, she could ask Jesus to make that snow globe go through walls or out the open doors onto the playground. They leave the doors open quite a bit now with the warm weather, especially after the janitor mops, you know, to dry the floor so no kids slip."

"Miss Maloney!" Detective Kurtz barked. "Are you saying Mary—the real Mary up in heaven—told Jesus to make the snow globe float off the shelf and down the hall and out the door and through the sky up into the hand of the Mary statue?"

"Why, I never thought of it, but if that's what you think, it could be possible."

"That is *not* what I think," Detective Kurtz huffed.

"Well, what do you think?" Mimi asked, turning to the priest.

Father Ernst leaned forward with his hands folded around the front knee of his crossed legs. "I think if Mary wanted to do that, of course, she could manage it. But tell me, Miss Maloney—"

"Oh, please, call me Mimi."

"Mimi, yes, why do you think she would want to do such a thing and cause so much disruption here at the school?"

Mimi looked at the Detective. He was behind the glare of the desk lamp, but she could see his face was getting red.

"I don't know. I think if Mary arranged the miracle she might have some message behind it. Maybe some symbolism."

"Symbolism?" Father Ernst asked, sounding intrigued.

"I'm not smart about these things, but maybe it stands for something she's trying to tell the parish, or maybe the whole world. But no one yet has been able to understand. Maybe if you could write a letter to the pope and get some of his top monks on it, they could pray and not eat meat for a while, and God would reveal to them what it's all about. But I don't' know. Like I said, I'm just an average girl."

"Tell me this," Detective Kurtz said slapping his open palm on the nurse's desk, "What do you know about the mailman getting robbed by two boys in masks outside your home?"

Mimi rubbed her chin thoughtfully. "Were they two boys? I hadn't heard that. My mother mentioned something about it at dinner last night. We had apricot chicken with rice and some of those rolls you have to crack the tube open on the countertop to make."

"It sounds delicious," Father Ernst said.

Detective Kurtz narrowed his eyes and cleared his throat.

"My mom's a really good cook. Maybe someday I can be like her and cook for my family."

"Who were these boys?" Detective Kurtz demanded, "Tell us now and it will mean a lot less trouble for you later."

Mimi shielded the light from her eyes to try to get a better look at Detective Kurtz behind the desk. "Oh, Detective, I swear, I don't know anything about that. I was at school all day yesterday. I only found out about it at dinner."

"Where did you say you're going to high school?" Father Ernst asked.

"Holy Footsteps."

"That's a fine school, and I'm sure you'll do well there. I have no further questions. Detective?"

Detective Kurtz moved the lamp light out of Mimi's eyes and trained it back on the desktop. He closed her file. "No further questions ... for now."

CHAPTER 20

SISTER MATHILDA SAT alone her room with the door closed, unable to see anything with the black patches on her eyes. The storm raging outside was pleasant, reassuring somehow. She thought about the Cutlass Supreme, her escape module to avoid retirement as soon as she could get her sight back and drive away. After she won it in the church raffle in 1966, it sat for a long time unused because even then her cataracts made the world a glaring blur. Once, though, on a summer night, Father Maligan called the nunnery from the priest house asking for Sister Mathilda. She came to the black wall phone in the kitchen by the icebox and said hello. In his nasally, mumbled brogue, he said something about a "chicken dinner" and wanting to borrow her car, because his wouldn't start. "That sounds wonderful," she said.

When he came by to get the keys, Father Maligan was confused that she followed him to the car and got in the passenger seat. "Let's go," she said. He started the engine and drove at speeds of 90 miles an hour with his window down and his pipe blazing to Collinsville, Illinois—across the Mississippi River—to Fairmount Park Race Track. There, they took their seats and he bought her an orange slushy and a large cup of Budweiser for himself. Unable to see much, Sister Mathilda thought at first he had surprised her and taken her to Busch Stadium for a Cardinals game. How thoughtful of him. What good fun. She kept asking who was pitching. Finally, she heard the pounding of horse hooves around the dirt track, and was aghast at this impropriety.

Father Maligan's horse, Chicken Dinner, came in fourth that night. It was the last time Sister Mathilda ever let anyone drive her Cutlass.

Thunder and lightening crackled outside her window. She noticed the lightening slightly through her black bandages and was tempted to take them off, even though removing them was forbidden. The doctor had warned her. "Whatever you do, don't take those bandages off early, or you might cause permanent damage." Her eyes needed total darkness for some time for her to see properly when they were healed.

"You can't trust doctors with your future," she thought.

She got up and made her way to the door and felt for the handle. She turned the bolt so no one would come in. Then counting the steps back to her dresser, as she had for years, she reached out her hand and touched the dresser top. She pulled out the second drawer and reached under it. Her fingertips found the Cutlass Supreme car title she had Scotch taped beneath the drawer. It was still there. She shut the drawer and felt her bandages.

"As soon as the doctor takes off your bandages," Sister Helen had told her, "we'll take you to the train station." But she knew what the principal meant. The train tracks led to the nursing home and the nursing home led to the cemetery.

Sister Mathilda closed her eyes tight and ripped off her bandages taking a few thick white eyebrow hairs with them. The room air was cool on her naked eyelids. She cupped her hands over her face and slowly opened her eyes. Light from the window and bedside lamp seeped through her fingers. Thunder rumbled. In sweet defiance to her doctor's orders, she slowly spread her fingers open all the way. Her pupils constricted. The window and rainy day outside came into view. She opened a drawer and got out six pair of old eyeglasses, trying on several until the trees sharpened into crisp focus. The operation had worked. She could see again as good as a young girl.

"Nursing home, my ass," she mumbled. Sister Mathilda moved closer to the window and watched the raindrops plopping in the mud puddles by the trees and the branches of bright green leaves bending in the wind, and the headlights of cars curving past the nunnery. There was a living world out there. After a while she went to the closet and got out her suitcase and packed it with an extra habit and some fresh stockings and underwear. Then she closed the suitcase and hid it under her bed. She put her eyeglasses back in the drawer, and put the bandages back on her eyes and smoothed out the adhesive tape to make it look undisturbed. Soon it would be time for lunch in the nunnery and she would count the steps to the kitchen and make herself a bologna sandwich with a glass of milk and some grapes to eat with the other nuns, and ask them to please describe what the outside world looks like today.

CHAPTER 21

TONY SAT DOWN in the interrogation chair. Father Ernst shut the door and once again took his seat on the sofa bench. Detective Kurtz turned the light in Tony's eyes, just like he'd done to Mimi. Tony squinted to get used to the light. He was a little nervous, but not like he would've been if he didn't have his love for Mimi. His love for Mimi was calming like the hot wine his parents let him sip once on Christmas Eve. Lately, he'd been thinking about her so much—even writing her name on scraps of paper—that he'd almost forgot he put the snow globe in Mary's hand. Mimi had told him to make up something for when they asked him who did it, and the night before, while reading his dad's copy of *The Godfather*, he had decided to blame the whole thing on the Mafia.

"Tony Vivamano, that's Italian," Father Ernst began.

"Yes, sir."

"Your ancestors came from Italy, and that is also where the Holy Roman Catholic Church is headquartered. Have you been to Rome?"

"No, sir."

"It's quite beautiful, the history, the art, the feeling of being close to God on earth."

"We went to the Wisconsin Dells over the summer. Have you ever been?

"I have not."

"Oh, you'd like it. They've got these bluffs that shoot out of the water and you can go on boat rides and see it all."

"I mentioned Rome only to remind you that your family, no doubt, has for generations been Catholic."

"Yes, sir."

"So, you no doubt, must feel a strong sense of faith, a strong sense of obligation to obey and support the church."

Tony shifted around a little. His parents and grandparents were all Catholic, and probably everybody going back to the boat and beyond. Sometimes his prayers worked, like when the hand grenade didn't blow up. But sometimes they didn't work, like when Brando died. So he wasn't sure what he felt toward the church, only that it was connected to the school and he was ready to move on to summer with Mimi and hanging out at the swimming pool. He was eager to shake off the hold that Mary Queen of Our Hearts had on his future. "I believe in God," he said.

"Tell us then, did you have anything to do with this snow globe getting up into the hand of Mary?"

"No, sir."

"Then why did you raise your hand?" said Detective Kurtz, leaning back in the creaking chair. Tony looked over at him and could see his badge shining behind the glare of the lamplight, but only the outline of his face was visible.

"Why did I raise my hand? That's a question I've been asking myself a lot lately."

"Tell us the truth," Father Ernst said reaching out to pat Tony on the knee. "All we want is the truth, right from your heart." Father Ernst got out a Pall Mall and lit it.

The room fell silent for a stretch. Tony smelled the smoke and thought about the truth, how he put the snow globe up there to offer up his troubles to Mary like a prayer. But that didn't have anything to do with why he raised his hand. He was thinking about a different truth. He decided it would look good, and come out easy, to share *that* truth with them.

"Father, have you ever been in love with a woman?"

Father Ernst coughed out all his smoke, and kept on coughing, thumping his chest to reset his entire system. Detective Kurtz looked over at him and waited. Tony waited. It was like a lung symphony, on and on. Finally, Father Ernst got his breath back, but spoke hoarsely. "Well, as you know, I have taken my vows, but I can say that as a younger man—"

"I don't see what this has to do with anything," Detective Kurtz interrupted. "Just answer the question. Why'd you raise your hand?"

"I did it for love," Tony said. The words in his mouth brought his feelings for Mimi gushing out in a tumble, like the scenic waterfall he had seen at the Wisconsin Dells. "I did it because I think I'm in love with Mimi Maloney, and I didn't want her to be in trouble alone."

Father Ernst and Detective Kurtz were quiet for a few seconds, exchanging investigative glances.

"That's a noble thing you did, to offer yourself up for her," Father Ernst said.

"Well, I can't stop thinking about her. I hope you won't tell anybody, but I can even see marrying her some day."

"Did she do it?" Detective Kurtz asked.

"Do what?"

Detective Kurtz shouted: "DID SHE PUT THE DAMNED SNOW GLOBE IN MARY'S HAND? YES OR NO?"

Tony leaned back in his chair. "I have no idea. I mean I don't think so." His voice was a little shaky from getting yelled at, but he thought of Mimi and calmed down.

"Well, what did she tell you about it?" Father Ernst asked gently.

"Not much. We didn't really discuss it. Oh, wait, I think she did say she thought it was a miracle. I don't know if I believe that. But who knows." Tony looked over at Detective Kurtz to see if he was going to yell again.

Detective Kurtz let out a gut sigh and slapped his Number Two pencil on the desktop. "Let's talk about what *you* think happened, Mr. Vivamano. How would you explain that snow globe getting up there?"

Tony took a breath and thought about the part of *The Godfather* in which the mob put a bloody horse head in someone's bed to send a warning. "Well, I have a theory," Tony said rubbing his hands together, "What if it has something to do with the archbishop? I mean, wasn't he at church the day it turned up?"

"The archbishop was there," said Father Ernst, "But surely you don't think he had anything to do with it."

"I don't know. I mean, I don't *think* he did it. For one, from what I've seen, he's not athletic enough. But what I'm thinking is maybe the archbishop is in some kind of trouble, maybe someone is out to get him, or at least send a warning to him that they know his schedule and they can reach out and touch him anytime they want."

"What are you saying?" Detective Kurtz said, "Who's out to get him?"

"The Mafia."

"That's ridiculous," Detective Kurtz said, "Why would the Mafia be after the archbishop?"

Tony turned to Father Ernst. "Father, have you ever heard the confession of somebody who was a criminal or maybe even killed somebody?"

"I can't say. It's forbidden for us to speak of such things."

"That's my point. Maybe the archbishop heard the confession of somebody the Mafia was after, and he told him all kinds of secrets, secrets the higher ups in the Mafia wanted to find out. But the archbishop refuses to tell them. Maybe the Mafia made a phone call and said, 'You think you're untouchable? Just look up in Mary's hand today after church.'"

Father Ernst folded his arms across his chest. "Well, that's an interesting theory, Mr. Vivamano."

"What about the mailman getting robbed in front of your girlfriend's house the other day," Detective Kurtz snapped out, "Was that the Mafia, too? Or did you have something to do with that?"

Tony raised his eyebrows together to look puzzled, but willing to help. "I'm sorry, sir, I don't know what you're talking about."

"You know. *You know I know you know*," Kurtz fumed.

Tony looked over at Father Ernst and held out his open hands, pretending to look for more information on the robbery. "What's he talking about, Father?"

"It's a separate case," Father Ernst said softly.

"Maybe not!" Detective Kurtz shouted. "Look, you can come in here with your love story and your Mafia yarn and your bullshit innocence, but I'm a law enforcement professional and I know."

Tony knew from playing Monopoly that when you land on somebody else's Boardwalk or Park Place that has some red hotels—unless you're stupid—you never want to raise your hand and admit your guilt. Let the other guy catch you on his property. Let the investigators prove he put the snow globe up there. He wasn't supposed to help them. He acted innocent and waited. The room was so quiet the only sound was Detective Kurtz drumming his fingernails on the desktop. Then it thundered outside in the distance.

"I think that will be all for now," Father Ernst said gently. He crushed out his cigarette in an ash tray. "Thank you, Mr. Vivamano."

"Oh, thank you, Father, and I hope you solve the case. Maybe ask the archbishop if he's heard any mob confessions lately."

Detective Kurtz studied Tony as he got up and walked out the door.

CHAPTER 22

FATHER MALIGAN FIRED Patrick and Tony as altar boys the day he caught them drinking the wine after 6:30 Mass. It was a September morning and they were in fifth grade. The scandal ended whatever hopes their mothers had of them becoming priests, but it also made them closer friends. They were both wearing long black altar boy robes with white smocks, standing in the green tile bathroom behind the altar preparing to rinse out the water and wine decanters. Usually there was some of the honey colored wine left after Mass. They were supposed to pour it back in the bottle, which was on the window ledge. But no wine was ever left in the decanter after a Father Maligan Mass. During the consecration of the Eucharist when the altar boys would pour the wine from the crystal decanters into the gold chalice, Father Maligan would always mumble urgently "pour it all in." A tall, big-boned man, Maligan had once been a football player in high school. Now in his late sixties, he had arthritic knees and drank for the pain. At the same time, he hated the bottle and lectured anyone in confession who admitted they got drunk.

"What was it like?" Tony asked.

"What do you mean?" Patrick said, rinsing out the decanters.

"When you kissed that girl in Michigan, how'd you talk her into it?"

"It took a lot of doing. First thing was—"

They heard Father Maligan coming. He was waddling on the tiled floor with his black wingtip shoes outside the bathroom, calling for them in his nasally voice, "Hey, you birds, where are you? What are you up to?"

Knowing Father Maligan was about to open the door, Patrick put down the decanter and grabbed the wine bottle to fool him. "I'll show him how to pour it all in," he said to Tony. Patrick gripped his hand around the bottleneck, hiding the cork, and held his fist to his mouth to look as if he were glugging it down. Father Maligan opened the door. His eyes widened when he saw the bottle in Patrick's mouth and Tony standing there next to him looking guilty.

"Patrick, you boozer, you're fired!" he said grabbing the bottle, "and just so there's no argument, your friend's fired, too."

"But the cork's in the bottle and I was just—" It was no use. Father Maligan walked away, taking the bottle with him, and Patrick and Tony changed back into their regular clothes and rode their bikes home never to serve Mass again.

The wine bottle incident was on Patrick's mind as he walked down the hallway to face his interrogation. Mimi had told him to make something up on his own to explain how he thought the snow globe got in Mary's hand. He had decided to blame it on Father Maligan.

"Mr. Cantwell, won't you please sit down," Father Ernst said.

Patrick sat in the chair and got the same bright light treatment from Detective Kurtz that Mimi and Tony had.

"You are the young man, if I recall correctly, who was reading a book on Dillinger," Father Ernst began. Father Ernst believed that a boy's book revealed a boy's heart. This was how he had solved the theft of the three wise men from St. James parish. In that case, his research had uncovered that one boy in the school—a heavy-set seventh grader—had checked out a book from the school library on the Lindbergh baby kidnapping. When the parish received a ransom note demanding twenty dollars and a jar of M&M's for the return of the wise men, Father Ernst soon got his confession. "Tell me, what do you know about Dillinger?"

Patrick's mind raced. He knew Dillinger had outsmarted the police most of the way, even escaping from jail with a wooden gun. It wasn't until the lady in red ratted on him that Dillinger got caught and shot down in the street outside a movie theatre. Probably, he should act casual about his interest in Dillinger, and not admit he felt sorry for him and wished he had gotten away and reformed on his own. The trick was to not get caught for the snow globe theft unless Tony got caught first for putting it in Mary's hand. That way they could run away together. Getting caught alone wouldn't do any good.

"Oh, I just started the book," Patrick said, "It has something to do with police working hard to catch some bad guy."

"I understand that where Dillinger is buried, his grave marker has often been stolen," Father Ernst said, "Some people admire him. They think of him as a Robin Hood. Do you admire him?"

"Robin Hood?"

"No, Dillinger, do you admire the exciting way he broke the law and often got away with it?"

"Me? No, I hope they catch him. But please, don't tell me how it ends."

"Do you believe the basic fact that no man can escape death? That someday we'll all have to face judgment?"

Patrick thought maybe a scientific answer to a religious question might throw him off. "I know that's one theory. But I also know a lot of our top scientists, men who can name all the planets, are working on cures all the time."

"A cure for death?" Father Ernst said.

"You never know."

Father Ernst shook his head and regrouped. "Tell me why you would choose to read this sort of book, a book about Public Enemy Number One, a bank robber."

"My Dad gave it to me for Christmas."

Detective Kurtz jumped in, cracking his knuckles and clearing his throat. "Are you in love with Mimi Maloney?"

Patrick felt his face get hot.

"You're blushing kid," Detective Kurtz said, "is that why you raised your hand, to protect her? Did she do it?"

"No, I don't think she did."

"So, why'd you raise your hand?"

Patrick told him the truth. "Because Tony's girlfriend broke up with him and his dog died."

Detective Kurtz and Father Ernst looked at each other.

"Tony was the second kid who raised his hand. Why did he raise his hand?" Kurtz asked.

"I don't know."

"Did he do it?"

Patrick laughed, a big fake laugh as loud as he could. Then he gulped some air down. "No, it wasn't Tony, believe me, if Tony did it I think I would know. Besides, he's very religious."

This seemed to interest Father Ernst. "What makes you say he's religious?"

"Oh, lots of things. Mostly, I guess, we were altar boys together, me and Tony, and he always got there on time, even for 6:30 Mass."

"Are you both still altar boys?"

"No, we moved on. I mean, they like to bring in some fresh talent."

"I see, well, how do you think the snow globe got up there in Mary's hand?" Father Ernst asked.

Patrick got set in his chair for the big lie. He wanted to look a little nervous to go with what he was about to say, but also he wanted to make sure he started right to look not too eager to say his theory. "I don't know if it's right for me to tell."

"Tell, what?" Detective Kurtz said, "Do you know who did it or not?"

"I know who did it."

Father Ernst and Detective Kurtz leaned forward. The room was crackling with anticipation. Finally a lead was about to emerge from a morning of fairy tales. Patrick could hear Father Ernst moving his tongue around in his mouth, like he was starving and somebody brought him a toasted sandwich jabbed with toothpicks and olives. Detective Kurtz started drumming his fingernails on the desktop with a snare-drum tension leading up to Patrick's answer.

"It was Father Maligan."

The investigators both reared back in disbelief. "Father Maligan? The old priest? What are you saying?" Detective Kurtz said smirking.

"How in heaven's name could this be possible?" Father Ernst said.

Patrick lowered his voice to a kind of secret fort whisper, so no one else in the world would be in on the secret except the three of them in the room. "Well, here's what I know. Along about Holy Week, maybe it was that day they wash your feet—"

"Holy Thursday?" Father Ernst said.

"That's right, it was on a Thursday. They had all of in class go over to the church for confession. Miss Kleinschmidt was with us and she went in first. She went in to tell her sins to Father Maligan. Now, I shouldn't say this, because it's probably wrong, but some of us near the door were listening to hear what she might say."

"Did you hear anything?" Detective Kurtz asked.

"Not right away. She was in there telling her sins real quiet and nobody knew what they were, except Father Maligan, because—"

Father Ernst bucked back and held up his open palm. "Please stop! Stop this very instant ... if you intend to reveal to us any of Miss Kleinschmidt's sins you overheard. It is against my vows to even talk of such things." He rubbed his face with his hand like a man whose vows were always after him.

Patrick looked at Detective Kurtz then back at Father Ernst. "OK, I won't tell you any of her sins, because really we couldn't hear any verbs. But we did hear her whispering away with her cigarette voice. She smokes quite a lot and sucks down coffee like a kitchen sink, so her voice kind of scratches your ears even when you can't hear the words."

"Get to the point," Detective Kurtz said.

"All of a sudden," Patrick whispered, "Father Maligan said to her, loud enough for everyone to hear it, 'WHAT DID YOU DO *THAT* FOR?'" Patrick leaned back, satisfied with his story so far.

"I don't see what any of this has to do with the snow globe," Father Ernst said winding his watch impatiently.

"It has to do with how she got real mad at him, telling him, '*Shhhhhhh.*' And then he said back to her, 'Do you want people to think you're a lush?' I asked Tony about that and he said that's somebody who gets drunk a lot. He's got an uncle—"

"Everybody's got an uncle, kid, but what does this have to do with the snow globe?" Detective Kurtz said.

Patrick drew a breath to make it sound awful. It was true, but he wanted to make it sound bad enough that Father Maligan might have put the snow globe in Mary's hand. "Well, then, we heard Miss Kleinschmidt say to him, real loud and bossy, 'I don't know why I even came to you. Everyone knows about you and your best friend, Jim Beam!' After that, she came out the door and went outside to smoke a cigarette and never did come back in to get her feet washed. And nobody would go to Father Maligan for confession, so he came out after a while, head down, and went back to the priest house. He was real sad. Everyone felt sorry for him."

"That's an interesting story, if it's true," Detective Kurtz said, "but are you saying that would make this old priest sneak into her classroom and—"

"He does have keys to the school."

"But why, pray tell, would he take Miss Kleinschmidt's snow globe and put it in Mary's hand?" Father Ernst asked. "What good would that do him?"

Patrick hadn't thought of that, so he nodded with chin in hand. "I don't know. Maybe just to get her in trouble for not keeping her desk decorations off the church roof."

Detective Kurtz groaned and pushed his chair back to stretch his legs. "OK, that's all for now," he said.

Patrick thanked them and got up to leave when Detective Kurtz threw out one last question. "What do you know about Richard Nixon?"

"Nixon?" Patrick thought of the Nixon mask he wore during the mailman robbery and his face got hot again. "He's in some kind of trouble, I heard, but I don't follow the news. It's too depressing." Detective Kurtz noticed him blush and picked up his pencil. Patrick nodded goodbye and opened the door and left. Detective Kurtz put a star by Patrick's name and wrote "mailman robber."

CHAPTER 23

MONSIGNOR O'DAY was alone in his room, practicing his tap dance number for the Mary Queen of Our Hearts Spring Follies. This year's musical, which O'Day had written himself, was about an Irish priest who prevents World War III by tap dancing before the United Nations. Kitchen calendars across the parish were marked for the event, because he had worked it into all his recent sermons. The show was an annual fundraiser in the gym with a cash bar and two intermissions, an evening of song and dance featuring Monsignor and the Mothers' Club volunteers.

Looking out his bedroom window while he danced, O'Day could see the rain falling on the empty blacktop playground. A reading lamp on his desk made the gold frame shine around a photograph of his late mother. She had white hair in a bun and smiling eyes that seemed to be watching her son's dance routine. With brisk footwork between the bookcase and the bed, Monsignor attempted a George M. Cohan kick off the wall.

He fell on the floor with a loud thud.

Before he could get up, there was a knock at the door.

"Are you all right in there?" It was Gerty the housekeeper wiping her hands on an apron and leaning into the door to hear if he was dying.

"I'm OK," O'Day said lying on the floor, "What is it?"

"You have a visitor," Gerty said.

He got up and put on his regular priest shoes and his black sports coat and went into the living room. Sitting on the edge of a green sofa in the sunken pit living room was a man who looked familiar. He wore a long blue raincoat, wet on the shoulders after walking in the rain from the car with no umbrella. His face was tired and he looked down at the rug. Monsignor O'Day couldn't remember who he was.

Mickey Riley was a former usher who had left the parish six years ago. Now, without warning, he was back to confess his sins and turn himself in. He stood up and they shook hands. Monsignor O'Day offered to take his coat. "I won't stay long," he said, "I don't deserve to take up your time." Monsignor sat down on the recliner next to him and tossed a TV guide with the Waltons smiling on the cover onto the end table next to a black telephone. They were alone. The room was lit by picture windows facing the prayer garden where Father Maligan practiced his nine iron shots on sunny days. But today the rain was falling on the window glass and the garden was empty and the room was dim and quiet. Above the stone fireplace was a modern art crucifix of made of twisted iron. There was no fire today. It hadn't been lit for a while.

"You may not remember me, but years ago I was an usher in the balcony."

"Ah! I remember you now. Mickey Riley, right?"

"Yes, that's right, Monsignor."

"How you been?"

"Well, not good. I'm here on a very grave matter."

"Is someone sick?"

"No."

"What is it?"

Riley rubbed his hands together and drew a big breath. "I want to turn myself in for what I did wrong. I was driving by the church looking for a sign for what to do and when I saw the police car out there—"

"Police car? Oh, that. Yes, we've had some trouble at the school."

"Well, maybe it's a sign, because when I saw that car, I knew I had to come admit to the crime."

Monsignor O'Day's eyes widened. He leaned forward and put his hand on Riley's shoulder.

"Was it you who put the snow globe up there?"

"I'm sorry, Monsignor, what?"

"Never mind," he said settling back. "What was it you wanted to confess?"

Riley started in on his sins, about how he used to be a good parishioner going to Mass with his wife, but then he bought a boat, a fourteen-foot long boat with an enclosed cabin. He kept it up at Alton harbor.

"Sounds like a lot of fun," Monsignor O'Day said.

"Well, it was at first, but boats are expensive." Riley explained how one Sunday when he was passing the collection basket in the balcony he realized he didn't have any money to fill up the boat that afternoon, so he borrowed a twenty-dollar bill from the basket. "I put it in my pocket when no one was looking as I was coming down the staircase from the balcony."

"So, the old balcony stair case trick?"

"What?"

"You're probably not the first one. But it was just a twenty, don't feel bad."

Riley cracked his knuckles and scratched his nose. "It wasn't just that one twenty. It was lots of twenties, and tens, and fives." He pulled an envelope out of his pocket and handed it to Monsignor O'Day. "I added it up to be about $600 worth of stolen cash over the years." He started crying. Monsignor O'Day looked at the envelope, which was quite wrinkled from being gripped with anguish. "I sold the boat. Now, I want you to call the police and turn me in," Riley said pointing to the phone. "I'll give the police a statement."

Monsignor O'Day picked up the phone. He dialed the number. "Hello, Gerty, what's for lunch?" He cupped the phone and turned to Riley. "She's making grilled cheese sandwiches with tomato soup. Is that okay?"

Riley nodded with his mouth open.

"Okay, Gerty, please make an extra lunch for our visitor, Mr. Riley. He's come to rejoin the parish." Riley took off his coat and followed Monsignor O'Day down a hallway.

For lunch they went into the dining room where Father Maligan was already seated slurping soup above a white-laced tablecloth. Monsignor O'Day didn't say anything to Maligan about Riley's confession. The three men talked about spring and baseball and what it would be like to be young again. "Those kids at the school here have it easy," Maligan said wolfing down his grilled cheese. "They've got nothing on their minds but having fun."

After lunch Monsignor O'Day walked Riley to the door to say goodbye. "Your sins are forgiven, but I haven't given you your penance yet."

"Anything, what is it?"

"Here." Monsignor O'Day gave him back the envelope full of money and told him to take his wife on a summer trip. "Maybe go down to the Ozarks, take her out to dinner, go dancing on one of those lakeside pavilions with the Japanese lanterns. You like dancing?"

"Edna does, but I'm not any good."

"Oh, I almost forgot, here, for you and Edna." He gave him two free tickets to the Spring Follies and told him the plot was about an Irish priest who prevents World War III by being such a good dancer. Then Monsignor O'Day did a little bit of his dance routine, but not enough to give away the show. Riley put the tickets in his pocket and hugged him. Monsignor O'Day shut the door and went back to his room and sat on his bed to switch back into his tap dance shoes to practice some more. Through the rain-drenched window, he noticed Riley dancing across a puddle to his car.

CHAPTER 24

FRIDAY ARRIVED WITH SUNSHINE and uncertainty. Sister Mathilda was harnessed to the clothesline walking back and forth plotting her escape. Through a gap in her bandage she could see blades of grass at her feet. Faking blindness she marched along mumbling, "Just a few more days." Her plan was to escape during the upcoming eighth grade graduation ceremony, two days ahead of her appointment to have her bandages removed. Her only concern was the Cutlass engine. Would it start? The last time she turned it over was midnight New Year's Eve. It made such a load roar that the next morning the principal, Sister Helen, started insisting Sister Mathilda get cataract surgery and make plans for the retirement home. That's when she hid the keys under the rock in a rosary pouch. The Saturday night Spring Follies would provide the diversion she needed to start the car unnoticed. "Just a few more days," she mumbled.

Mimi, Tony, and Patrick walked out on the playground talking in low tones about how well the counter investigation was going—maybe too well. It felt as though the whole thing could fall apart at any moment.

"If they find out," Patrick whispered to Tony, "meet me at the bridge and we'll run away from there."

Tony didn't answer. He was looking at the top button on Mimi's blouse.

"It's gorgeous out," Mimi said skipping. The boys watched her lead the way onto the hot, crowded playground. Some of the eighth grade boys were playing Kill the Man with the Ball. It was a forbidden game that came out of nowhere that spring. Ignoring the neat yellow stripes painted on the blacktop to contain each class in designated corners, a daring boy would grab one of the maroon kickballs and yell, "Kill the man with the ball!" With that, everyone on the playground would stop what they were doing and chase after him. The goal was to tackle the man with the ball and pile up on top of him.

Jimmy Purvis, a lean eighth grader and one of the highly respected Gang of Five who had run away in fifth grade, was weaving through the crowd with the ball. Kids from every grade, boys and girls, were rushing toward him with a joyous blood lust. Mothers' Club volunteers yelled, "Let's have peace!" But no one heard them. How could they? Kill the Man with the Ball was primordial and unstoppable. The only way to escape ending up at the bottom of the pile was for the fleeing student to toss the ball to someone else at the last second. Jimmy ran by and tossed the ball to Patrick.

"Run!" Mimi yelled.

Patrick took off with Mimi chasing after him and Tony chasing after her. The three of them ran astride flicking the ball to each other when tacklers lunged.

Detective Kurtz and Father Ernst stepped outside for some fresh air and noticed the commotion. Standing by the dumpster, Detective Kurtz took a fresh red pack of Dentyne gum from his shirt pocket and put a piece in his mouth. Father Ernst lit up a Pall Mall and watched the game.

The darting, dodging, and passing of Mimi, Patrick, and Tony defied the mob.

"No one can catch us!" Mimi yelled to Patrick as he gave her the ball. And it seemed no one could. The pyramid system of getting all the students to repeat two main theories was working. One student after another had faced Father Ernst and Detective Kurtz, telling them either the snow globe in Mary's hand was a miracle somehow, or maybe Miss Kleinschmidt put it up there. But the investigators standing on the playground watching Kill the Man with the Ball had noticed a pattern. All of the students except the first three gave answers that were artless and brief, suggesting they had nothing to hide and were just following a script. But who wrote the script? Whose answers stood out? Mimi Maloney, Tony Vivamano, and Patrick Cantwell. Their performances had been so richly detailed, it made them look guilty by contrast. The problem for the investigators was they had no evidence.

"Oh, hell!" Tony yelled tossing the ball to Patrick.

A row of seventh graders swung like a cemetery gate on Tony, Patrick, and Mimi. Down they went. Patrick held the ball. Mimi fell on top of him and Tony on top of her. They gulped their final breaths and waited for the pain of the pile up. Ten students dove on, then fifteen, twenty and thirty. At the bottom of the pile they could only suffer and wait. Bodies blocked the sunlight. The tangle of legs and arms and school uniforms muffled the happy screams of students at the top jumping on. Under the tonnage, vital organs waited for blood no longer circulating. When would it end? When would they unload? Lungs burned like swimmers underwater who couldn't come up for air. There was no breathing, only the holding of breath at the very bottom. To exhale was to feel your lungs collapse under the push of bodies above you, and there was no drawing a second breath at the bottom.

"GET OFF!" yelled a Mothers' Club guard, running up. She grabbed students by the arms and peeled them off the top of the heap. "Someone could get killed!"

"It's Kill the Man with the Ball," Jimmy Purvis told her.

Detective Kurtz and Father Ernst watched from a distance as Mimi, Patrick, and Tony wobbled back to their feet. The three of them laughed and smiled at each other. Detective Kurtz chewed his gum between his front teeth and looked over at Father Ernst. He nodded in agreement. It seemed Mimi, Patrick, and Tony were a unit. Somehow, they were in cahoots, but how was not yet clear. They decided to work privately on the case over the weekend and meet again next week to solve the crime.

CHAPTER 25

SATURDAY MORNING Mimi got on her green Schwinn with the white basket and rode over to Patrick's house. She asked him if he wanted to go on a bike ride.

"Sure. Where to?"

It was a surprise, she said, but first they had to go get Tony. Tony was glad to see them. He sneaked away from doing dishes and off they went, two boys following Mimi to see where she would take them. They rode for a long while, watching Mimi in her pink short pants in front of them, her hair floating in the wind. Tony was right behind her, close enough to smell the Charlie perfume she had used that morning.

Mimi was the central figure in a breezy watercolor painting, Spring Day with Girl on a Bike. The background changed as they rode through neighborhoods. Green lawns, yellow forsythia bushes, deep red tulips flew by, but the boys gazed only at Mimi in the wild, bright center of the painting. It was good to see her out of school and out of uniform. When they got to the stoplight by the HiPointe Theatre, they saw Forest Park across the street and Tony figured out where she was taking them.

"The zoo? You're taking us to the zoo?"

Mimi nodded. "I decided you've both been working so hard, you deserve that field trip."

The boys looked at each other. They should have been happy. But instead, they were uneasy. Both wished they were alone with Mimi. Both wished they were on a date with her and could park their bikes and walk all over the zoo holding hands with her, and then kiss her over and over again under some tree. Kissing Mimi felt like an imperative. Their blood warmed. They were under a mandate of nature—kiss the girl in the painting.

"This sounds like a lot of fun," Patrick said blankly, feeling he had to say something.

"Yeah, this will be great," Tony said, taking a deep breath that told his DNA to wait patiently for the chance to kiss her.

The light turned green and Mimi pushed off toward Forest Park and the waiting zoo with the boys riding right behind her. A black VW waited at the light and then followed slowly behind them. Father Ernst adjusted his sunglasses and pushed up the sleeves of his light blue sweater. He was working the case on his day off, armed with a 35-millimeter camera and a zoom lens.

Patrick kissed Mimi first. It happened near the tiger cages when Tony wasn't looking. A Bengal tiger paced back and forth snarling at the zoo visitors, his claws clacking on the cement floor every time he did the turn around. The tiger in the cage wanted to get out; Patrick could see it in his eyes. That tiger was like his secret crush on Mimi. The tiger wanted to leap and roar and be free. He wanted to be a *real* tiger, not a caged attraction performing for the tourists.

Mimi was standing right next to Patrick, and Tony had stepped away to a private area to fan away some gas after eating a piece of cold pepperoni pizza for breakfast. Mimi's lips were profiled against the tiger cage. Back and forth, back and forth ... Patrick was looking at the tiger and then at her lips. When she turned to say something to him, he pounced.

Father Ernst—lurking unnoticed on the opposite side of the cage—pushed the button on his camera as Patrick's lips met Mimi's. *Click.* It was now evidence in the case.

"What are you doing?" Mimi asked.

Patrick heard the question and knew right away he had no good answer. "I don't know," he said, looking back at the tiger. *How could he have done such a thing?* Right away, he blushed, embarrassed and ashamed. He had betrayed his friendship with Tony like it was nothing. He hated himself and got quiet.

"You guys are my two favorite people in the world," Tony said walking up. He hadn't seen what happened. He put his arms on their shoulders.

"Let's ride our bikes some more," Mimi said. "Around the park."

They ended up on the top of Art Hill, by the Art Museum where Patrick went inside to use the bathroom. That's when Tony struck. He kissed Mimi as they stood by their bikes beneath the statue of The Thinker.

Father Ernst got a picture of that, too. He was leaning by the Statute of King Louis XIV on horseback, sword in the air. No one saw him. Tony tried to kiss her a second time, but she turned away.

"What are you doing?" Mimi said.

"What am I doing?" Tony laughed. He was enjoying a love feast in a starving land. He pointed to the statue. "I'm doing what he told me to do."

Mimi looked up at The Thinker. He seemed to know the heart of every mortal who passed by. He knew that for Mimi, kissing Patrick and Tony was boring, like tasting some goulash recipe on a spoon her mother would stick in her face when she wasn't hungry. She had no interest in kissing boys. Not today. She had done plenty of kissing, and more, with her boyfriend on the golf course. After the hand grenade incident, all she wanted to give Patrick and Tony was her friendship and thanks for saving her life. There was more to life than kissing. There was something you couldn't see unless you were blind, something you couldn't afford unless you were broke, something you couldn't know you already owned unless you almost lost it. If only the stone lips of The Thinker could move. He would tell the boys that Mimi had reckoned herself dead, and reckoned it wrong, and woke up to be alive again.

"Why don't you guys go on without me," Patrick said. He walked out of the Art Museum ready to go home. He had washed his face in the bathroom and resolved to bow out.

Mimi looked at Patrick. "We need to stick together. I have something to tell you about tonight."

"Tonight?"

"Wait," Tony said touching Mimi's shoulder, "I got something to say."

Mimi and Patrick looked at him.

"Mimi, will you be my date at the graduation dance?"

His date? Tony was so eager, she didn't want to hurt his feelings. She looked at both boys, then rested her gaze on Tony. "Would that make you happy?"

"Yeah," Tony said.

Mimi looked at Patrick and he blinked, a letting-go blink.

"All right then, Mr. Vivamano," she said in a playful formal tone, "I will be your date at the graduation dance." She held out her hand and curtsied. Tony dumped his bike and danced with her beneath the statue. Patrick watched and felt better about it all, but at the same time, he realized his plan of escaping the future on a freight train with Tony was slipping away.

CHAPTER 26

MIMI WAS OUT RIDING her bike when Detective Kurtz parked his patrol car in front of her house and got out. He stood there, chewing on a piece of spent gum, hitching up his weapons belt, and looked around. It was a fine spring day. Birds singing. Lawnmowers humming. He looked up the hill of the front lawn where the two masked boys had robbed the mailman. This was it. This was where he was going to crack the snow globe case. He could feel it. This was the day he was going to start solving all the other nagging juvenile crimes in this sector. He spit out his gum and walked toward the house. The gravel crunched under his shiny black shoes as he walked up the driveway and rang the doorbell. He pushed so eagerly on the button it left a little dent on his fingertip.

Inside, Mimi's older sister was practicing Chopin's funeral march. Mrs. Maloney was in the kitchen chopping green peppers to mix into a bowl of ground beef for tonight's barbecue.

"I'll get it," Mrs. Maloney said wiping off her hands and rushing to the door. She opened it and saw a police officer.

"Ma'am."

She brushed away a strand of hair from her face with her backhand. "Yes?"

Detective Kurtz introduced himself and said he was following up on the mailman robbery. "May I come in?"

"Well, my husband's not home. He went to get a baseball glove with our son," she said. "He outgrew his last glove over the winter. Do you need to talk to both of us?"

"No, it's nothing formal," he said, "just a visit."

"Well, alright. Would you like something to drink, some water or anything?"

"No, thank you, ma'am. I won't stay that long."

She closed the door behind him and led him to the dining room table. Mimi's sister looked up and saw it was a police officer, but kept on playing the funeral march.

"I have a few questions," he said sitting down at the head of the table.

"Glad to help," she said straightening up some junk mail on the table.

"I see your mail is coming again."

"Oh, just like always. It never stopped. We even got our mail that day."

Detective Kurtz perked up. This was new information. "You did?"

"Yes, although my husband joked he wished they had stolen our bills." She laughed like they were getting to know each other at the parish progressive dinner party. But Detective Kurtz didn't laugh back, so she stopped.

"Why your house, Ma'am?"

"You mean, why'd they rob the mailman here?"

"Yes, that's what I'm curious about."

"Well, I don't know," she said raising her voice over a flourishing passage of the funeral march. It sounded as though a black casket were being carried through a Polish village with mourners lining the cobblestone sobbing. "I guess it was just a coincidence. There's nothing of value in our mail."

"Your daughter is Mimi? Mimi Maloney?"

"Yes," she said touching her collarbone with a hint of concern. "Do you know my Mimi?"

"No, I don't think I do." That was a lie. If asked later why he lied, Detective Kurtz could always say he didn't think he knew the real Mimi, only the Mimi who had spun fairy tales in a school interrogation. "How's Mimi doing in school?"

Mrs. Maloney leaned back and beamed a relaxed smile. "Oh, she's doing great. She got accepted to Holy Footsteps Academy and she's just wrapping up eighth grade."

"Has Mimi told you anything about how school is going these days?"

"No, nothing's happening. No big tests anymore. These are the dull last days before the summer and then she can start a new life in the fall."

Detective Kurtz nodded. Obviously, Mimi had not told her mom about the snow globe investigation. "Is Mimi home now?"

The Chopin funeral march had reached a middle section of graceful runs and romantic chords recalling a spring day on which a girl like Mimi might run through fields of flowers, far, far from death. "No, Mimi's not in. She went on a bike ride."

"It's such a nice day for it."

"Yeah, I told her to go someplace nice, but she said she was going to go to the library to study."

Detective Kurtz nodded. "Did you say the mail came for you the day of the robbery?"

"Yes."

"May I see what came that day? I mean, do you still have it?"

Mrs. Maloney got up and rooted around the buffet top. "When was that?"

"Wednesday."

"We get so much mail, none of it any good. Oh, here we go." She wheeled around and handed him the stack of bills and the letter from Holy Footsteps Academy.

Detective Kurtz glanced at the bills, set them aside, and pulled out the fake letter from Holy Footsteps Academy.

"We threw away a letter you would probably love to see, to help you solve the crime."

He stopped reading and looked up. "What letter?"

"It was a chain letter, a pyramid scheme that said we should send a dollar to a lot of people and say the Hail Mary and that something good would happen to us if we obeyed, and something bad would happen if we didn't."

"What'd you do with it?"

"My husband threw it away," she said shaking her head. "So far, nothing bad has happened."

Detective Kurtz nodded and went back to reading Mimi's fake letter from Holy Footsteps Academy—the one saying they were looking forward to her arrival in the fall. He looked at the letterhead and content and signature. It seemed authentic. He folded it and slid it back in the envelope and looked at the address.

Then he saw it.

The postage stamp wasn't properly canceled. Not by a machine. It looked as though someone had drawn wiggly lines on it with a blue ink pen. This was not right. He didn't know what it meant, but this was significant. This was evidence and it was tied to Mimi. His heart beat faster.

"Did this come in the mail that day?"

"Yes."

"Well, you must be very proud of Mimi. That sounds like a good school."

"Oh yes, Mimi's sister goes there." Turning to the piano she called out, "Can't you play something more cheerful?" The funeral march was back to the main refrain, the part that sounds like "Pray for the dead and the dead will pray for you."

"May I please borrow this letter for our investigation?"

"Why, I don't know why not … if you think it might be important."

"It's probably nothing."

"Well, okay, if it will help you catch these robbers, you can have it. Do you also want the Laclede Gas bill?"

"No, ma'am, I got enough bills of my own." They both laughed, and Detective Kurtz got up. Mrs. Maloney showed him to the door, and he walked to his car trying very hard not to smile. It was a very fine spring day.

CHAPTER 27

THAT NIGHT THE GYMNASIUM was packed. Hundreds of adults sat in rows of metal folding chairs, waiting in the dark on the basketball court. Stage lights played on the red velvet curtains. The floor was sticky from slopped drinks, held in plastic cups by parents happier than they had been all week around their desks and dishwashers. A large, cheerful woman in pink dress sat before the upright piano down in front. The crowd applauded. She smiled and played a few exciting chords. Monsignor O'Day wandered out in front of the curtain, pretending to be lost. "Is this 10:30 Mass? I've never seen such a crowd." Everyone laughed and applauded. He apologized for his limited talents, but promised that the Mothers' Club volunteers would carry the show. Then it was time for the national anthem. A row of cub scouts marched up the middle aisle in blue shirts and yellow neckerchiefs and put the flag in a gold stand. The piano player gave the introduction and everyone stood up with their hands on their hearts. Father Ernst was there next to an empty chair reserved for Detective Kurtz, who was running late. Miss Kleinschmidt limped in the gym as the crowd began to sing.

"Oh, say can you see ..."

Running through dark back yards, Mimi, Patrick and Tony flanked around the rear of school. Mimi had a plan—to sneak into their classroom and set a booby trap for Miss Kleinschmidt. "It will help with the investigation," she claimed. The boys obeyed. After kissing her that morning,

Tony just wanted to be with her again. Patrick went along hoping somehow they'd get caught. That way he and Tony could run away. The gold statue of Mary glowed in a spotlight against the first stars of a clear night. Parked cars packed the playground where just the other day kids had played Kill the Man with the Ball.

"Look who's coming," Mimi whispered.

Sister Mathilda walked out of the nunnery on Sister Helen's arm, making her way past the parked Cutlass and up the exterior stone steps to the gymnasium.

"You have a good sense of balance for someone who can't see at all," the principal said.

"I couldn't make it without you," Sister Mathilda said. In her pocket was her secret rosary pouch with the keys to the Cutlass. She had retrieved it earlier in the day during her afternoon walk on the dog run line, and held the key under hot water in her bedroom, drying it off to get it good and clean for the moment of ignition. Her plan was to excuse herself to use the restroom during some interesting part of the show, when no one else would leave, so she could slip out to start the car and make sure the engine was ready for her approaching escape.

"O'er the lan-yand of the freeeeeeeee … and the home of the brave!"

Everyone clapped and sat back down and slugged back some more alcohol and jostled around to get comfortable for the show. This was it. The piano player started thumping her feet and plunking out some Irish chords, as the curtain rose. Scene One was an Irish village where the young priest played by Monsignor O'Day, wearing a black wig, sat on a stone well, talking to some farm girls played by three Mothers' Club volunteers in Irish dresses and red pigtail wigs.

"Father, it's nice of you to stop and draw water for us," a farm girl said, "but what we really want to know is how to dance."

"Oh, no I couldn't," Monsignor O'Day said, "I'm on duty."

"Oh, c'mon, no one will know," they all said.

The crowd applauded. Monsignor O'Day got up from the well. "OK, if you promise not to tell the archbishop, I'll show you one little ditty."

At that, the piano player rolled into an Irish jig and the crowd clapped to the beat. O'Day danced back and forth, kicking his legs, twirling from arm to arm with different farm girls. Their red pigtails swung over their shoulders.

Everyone was having a good time and then, the archbishop arrived on stage, played reluctantly by Father Maligan wearing long green vestments and a pointed hat.

"O'Day! You boozer, what are you doing? I should fire you!"

The piano player drummed some dramatic minor chords and the crowd laughed.

"I haven't been drinking," O'Day told the archbishop, "I was just showing these girls the joy of the faith."

"Well, that's joy enough. Get back to work, and you girls move it along, a storm's coming."

The farm girls held out their hands and looked at the sky.

"But Archbishop, there are no clouds," a farm girl said. "What storm?"

"Don't you birds read the paper? The storm clouds of war!"

Father Maligan got a cheat sheet from his pocket to read the lyrics to his song, which he had failed to memorize. The delay prompted O'Day to look at his watch and ad lib, "He'll find his spot in a minute … it's just like 6:30 Mass."

The crowd laughed.

Maligan frowned but kept going. The piano player vamped into Maligan's song, a minor maelstrom of approaching armies that no man could stop.

Meanwhile, outside, Mimi, Patrick, and Tony spied from the edge of the fence toward the entrance to the gym. They could see a few parents smoking at the top of the exterior stone staircase. The orange tips of their cigarettes glowed as they watched the show through the open door. "We can't go in that way," Mimi whispered, "Nobody can know we were here."

"Right, let's try the side doors," Tony said.

They darted through the shadows around the nunnery toward the school, checking doors, but finding them all locked. When they saw a second-story boys' restroom window open a crack—above the bike racks—Mimi told Patrick and Tony to lean one of the bike racks against the building as a ladder. It was twenty-foot long heavy metal rack, but the boys hoisted it against the stone wall beneath the window.

"Ladies first," Tony said with a sweeping gesture from Mimi up the ladder.

Up she went, with the boys watching her butt as she reached the window. To Tony, it was a moment of pure butt. But to Patrick, it was butt mixed with sadness. If it weren't for that butt, he thought, and all of Mimi's other charms and schemes, he and Tony would probably have been caught by now for the snow globe theft, and they'd have left town on a freight train. As Mimi pushed the window open wider, wriggling around talking bossy to it—"Get up now, I'm in charge"—Patrick felt he had not only betrayed Tony by kissing her, but also betrayed his own longstanding engagement to the tracks.

The problem was that sometimes around Mimi, Patrick couldn't even remember his feelings for the tracks. To be near Mimi made the idea of running away on a boxcar seem pointless. By kissing her, he had taken a step toward being an ordinary boy—a boy who would go to high school, then college, and get married. Maybe even get a job downtown. Mimi was a dangerous girl to be around.

"How's it comin' up there, babe?" Tony called up the ladder.

Babe?

Patrick realized—again—that unless they got caught and soon, there was little hope of Tony ever running away with him.

"I got it," she whispered. Her arms pushed up the window and she pulled herself into the dark boys' room. Then her face popped out grinning down on the boys. "C'mon."

Tony climbed up first eager to ascend the ladder to Mimi. Then it was Patrick's turn. He got about halfway up, when he noticed the headlights of a car swinging in the driveway in the front of the school. It was a police car headed his way. Patrick considered—for a split second—lagging behind to get caught. But that was no good. What he needed was to get caught with Tony. Patrick squirreled up to the top.

The patrol car, driven by Detective Kurtz, cruised up the driveway toward the bike racks. Kurtz was chewing gum, listening to the police radio for any fresh dispatches on juvenile crime, when he looked over and saw the bike rack leaning against the building. That's odd. His eyes ran up the ladder and caught the flash of a boy's tennis shoe flitting in the window.

CHAPTER 28

"IT'S THEM," Detective Kurtz said. Whipping his patrol car to a stop, he got out and ran over to the bike rack and started to climb up. Inside the dark Boys room, Mimi, Tony, and Patrick spied down on him and looked at each other. They knew what to do without saying it. All three of them reached up and shut the window, then Mimi locked it.

"Damn." Detective Kurtz scampered backwards, but his weight was too much. The bike rack skidded down the side of the building and flopped him on the ground. He sprung up cursing. His elbow in a short-sleeved shirt was scraped bloody. "Tonight's the night you little bastards."

"We better move fast," Mimi said. She darted out of the restroom with the boys right behind her. The hallway was dark except the red Exit light reflecting on the polished tile floor. They hurdled up the staircase, laughing and cussing and almost tripping, toward Miss Kleinschmidt's room on the top floor.

Sitting in the back row of the gym, Miss Kleinschmidt reached in her purse to get a cigarette to smoke outside. Her fingers rooted through makeup and keys and used Kleenex, while Monsignor O'Day—up on the stage—was in a battle scene in the trenches hearing the confession of a soldier.

"I'm afraid I might end up killing somebody, somebody just as scared as me on the other side," the soldier said.

"There's only one way to stop this terrible war," O'Day told the soldier.

"What, prayer?"

"No, someone has to get out there between the trenches and dance."

The crowd applauded. The nicotine receptors in Miss Kleinschmidt's brain were on high alert, having already been activated by the sound of her rooting through her purse. She really wanted a smoke now. But the pack in her purse was empty. She got up and decided to go to her classroom for the school pack she kept in her desk drawer.

Up on the stage, the soldiers from the trenches lowered their rifles to watch the priest dancing in the no-man's land between them.

"Come out boys and join me," O'Day called out. "The war can wait."

A lone soldier laid down his rifle and crawled out of the trenches to dance, then another and another. Detective Kurtz rushed up the exterior steps into the gym. He was panting as he glanced at the stage and observed the foolishness all around him. The audience in the dark was laughing and clapping, the piano player plinking out happy chords, while a row of soldiers danced arm in arm with Monsignor O'Day.

"Madness," Kurtz muttered. He walked into the gym, knowing the boy who climbed in the window was either Patrick or Tony. Or maybe he just saw the shoe of the last one. Hell, they could all three be roaming around ripe for arrest. Breaking and Entering. Trespassing. Charges like that could wrench out a confession on the snow globe—and plenty of other juvenile crimes in the area. Striding into the dark gym, he had to make a decision. He had to think like they would think. Where would they be going right now in this big wide school? Either one of two places. Either into Miss Kleinschmidt's class. He looked up near the ceiling at the row of picture windows above the gym, the windows that ran along the hallway leading to Miss Kleinschmidt's class. If they were going there, he knew he would see them running past the windows. His eyes squinted. Nothing.

Mimi, Patrick, and Tony crawled on the hallway floor beneath the windows.

Or, Detective Kurtz thought, they could be breaking into the interrogation room to try to rifle through some papers and mess with the investigation. That's it! That's where they were headed. Detective Kurtz pushed through the crowd, spilling drinks, and went into the interrogation room and closed the door and sat behind the desk with the light off. He pointed the dark desk lamp at the doorway like a loaded gun ready to shoot the glaring bulb at the guilty bastards when they sneaked in.

Sister Mathilda could hear the crowd cheering and laughing as Monsignor O'Day danced with the soldiers.

"I'm going to use the restroom now," she whispered to Sister Helen sitting next to her.

"It's so dark, you want me to go with you?"

"No, thank you, I'm used to the dark. I know my way around."

The principal nodded and went back to watching the show. Sister Mathilda unpeeled the adhesive from the bottom of her black cataract eye patches, so she could see the floor. She bumped into someone.

"Excuse me."

"No, pardon me." It was Miss Kleinschmidt headed through the same doorway into the first floor hallway. She recognized Sister Mathilda by her black habit in the dark. "Where you going? You need some help?"

"No, thanks, I'm just going to the little girls room. Where you going?"

"Oh, I just thought I'd check my classroom for some papers I forgot."

They parted ways, Sister Mathilda clutching the rosary bag with the Cutlass keys in it, and Miss Kleinschmidt gripping her cigarette lighter.

Kneeling on the floor with Tony and Patrick behind her, Mimi grabbed the doorknob to Miss Kleinschmidt's classroom. It swung right open. She stuck her fingernail in the door jam and plucked out the wadded-up paper towel scrap she had put in there as she left Friday afternoon. "Let's get in and get out," she said.

Patrick whispered to Tony. "If anybody sees us, run for the tracks. Meet on the bridge."

"We won't get caught," Tony said. He had full confidence in Mimi.

Inside the class, they stood up and gently closed the door. It clicked shut. They turned to face the empty desks. Their prison cell looked different at night. The only light came from the three full-length windows facing the front lawn, where floodlights shooting up at the school threw cemetery shadows from the tombstone rows of empty desks. To be standing there beyond the school day without Miss Kleinschmidt vexing them, they were like three grade school ghosts drifting through a room that no longer held any power over them. Soon it would feel like this forever, when the last bell would ring and the room would empty out.

"I say we trash this place and pee on her desk," Tony said.

Mimi and Patrick looked at him. But before they could answer, they heard applause and saw a light in the hallway. It was coming from the windows overlooking the gym. The gym lights were on. They listened and heard adults talking and laughing.

"Must be intermission," Mimi said.

"Wait," Patrick said snapping his fingers.

They listened again and heard footsteps right outside the door, and then the sound of a key chain jangling at the lock. It was Miss Kleinschmidt.

Sister Mathilda put the cataract eye patch in her habit pocket and peeked her head out of the Girls restroom into the hallway. All clear. She scurried past the knee-high drinking fountain and down a fight of steps to the exit doors. There she paused to kick the throw rug into the door so it wouldn't lock behind her. With a quick glance left and right, she swept down the outside steps into the night. Her Cutlass was waiting.

Father Ernst reached for the doorknob outside the interrogation room. He, too, was hunting for a pack of cigarettes and remembered he'd left one on the leather couch. As he opened the door, he heard a voice from the darkness.

"You're under arrest," Detective Kurtz said, switching on the lamp.

The desk lamp blasted him with light and Father Ernst fell backwards into the interrogation chair.

"Shit, it's you," Detective Kurtz said. "I thought you were them."

"Them?"

"Them, dammit! They're in the school somewhere."

"Who?"

"I'm not sure, but I saw a boy's shoe going in a window. Run upstairs to Kleinschmidt's room and have a look around for anything unusual. I'll stay here."

Detective Kurtz switched off the lamp—but not before Father Ernst noticed a dab of blood on the desktop from Kurtz's elbow. He shut the door and ventured out into the dark, first floor hallway.

Miss Kleinschmidt opened the door to her classroom and flipped on the lights. The room was empty. She sniffed the air and moved along the first row of desks toward her own desk to get some cigarettes. Mimi, Patrick, and Tony were crouched behind the bookcase in the corner. They couldn't see her, but they could hear her. Her warden shoes clopped to a stop and then a desk drawer opened. It was quiet and then they heard a cigarette lighter flicking. They heard her breathe in and exhale with relief, and then she started talking to herself.

"The dancing priest! Shit, I could dance every bit as good if I wanted to."

Mimi, Patrick, and Tony looked at each other, then turned their heads again to listen. They could hear Miss Kleinschmidt dancing around by her desk. She was tapping along just like Monsignor O'Day. She was pretending that she was in the play, that she was preventing World War III. "I'll show them all," she mumbled. Her shoes clunked along in the dark, scuffing up the floor, and then she went into a coughing fit and sank into a student's desk.

There was a knock at the door.

"Who is it?" Miss Kleinschmidt called out, getting up.

"It's me ... Father Ernst, are you all right?"

Sister Mathilda got behind the wheel of her Cutlass. She looked through the windshield, imagining the open road leading west to visit her sister and see her parent's grave. With a shaky hand, she slipped the key in the ignition, pumped the gas pedal, and turned the key.

The 320 horsepower, Jetfire Rocket V8 engine awoke, shooting black smoke out the tailpipe.

Miss Kleinschmidt opened the door a crack, holding her cigarette behind her back. Father Ernst smelled it right away.

"Father, what are you doing out there in the dark?"

"I was at the show and there's been some funny business. Kids in the school. Detective Kurtz suggested I have a look around."

Miss Kleinschmidt flicked the ashes on the cigarette behind her back, wanting him to leave. "Nothing going on up here."

"May I borrow a cigarette?"

She put the cigarette in her mouth, took a drag, and opened the door all the way. "Come on in."

As he entered, Father Ernst scanned the room, looking for some sign of intruders. He peeked his head in the cloakroom and saw nothing but empty hooks.

"Nobody's here but us," Miss Kleinschmidt said. "The door was locked when I came in."

"That's good." She gave him a Benson and Hedges, not his brand, but still a smoke. He lit up and looked about the room some more, noticing the bookcase in the corner. The books attracted him. He walked toward the bookcase while he smoked.

"I hope you catch those little shits, excuse my French, Father," she said, "I mean, what nerve, if it is them, sneaking in the school on a night like this."

Mimi, Patrick, and Tony looked at each other as they heard the footsteps of Father Ernst approaching. Patrick considered the possibility, the glorious possibility, that they were about to get caught. He envisioned all three of them knocking over Father Ernst and running out the door for the tracks. There, he and Tony could kiss Mimi farewell and leave on the first slow freight. Father Ernst stopped. He was so close they could taste his cigarette. But he wasn't looking behind the bookcase. He was looking at the books in the bookcase.

"You never really know what they're learning, what they're really thinking at this age," he said.

"Who?"

"Eighth graders."

"Hmmmph," she said looking at her empty desks. "I know what they're thinking. They're thinking of themselves, how they can get through life easy without having to keep their promises or make any commitment. All they want is pleasure and to mock authority, mock teachers, mock the church." She wandered over to her snow globe and wound it up and put it on her desk.

"I didn't know it was musical," Father Ernst said. He walked away from the bookcase and looked at the snow globe, which was swirling with snowflakes from being disturbed. "What that song?"

"You know, 'Love Me Tender'."

They both smoked and watched it for a few puffs. Miss Kleinschmidt smoldered at the memory of the man who gave it to her and quit writing, never called. She picked it up after a few stanzas and stuffed it back on the shelf where the song wound down and ended abruptly. "Are you gonna catch these little bastards, for what they did to me, or what?"

Father Ernst flinched. "We will. We have some good leads."

"I should hope so. Time is short."

"You're right. I'd better go. Better have a look around the rest of the school. Thanks for the smoke."

"Sure."

Mimi, Patrick, and Tony kept hidden, listening to the sound of Miss Kleinschmidt unwrapping a fresh sleeve of crackers. She was munching away at her desk when the music from the Spring Follies started back up and the crowd downstairs in the gym applauded. She put away the crackers, got up, turned off the lights, and shut the door behind her.

CHAPTER 29

MONSIGNOR O'DAY'S big scene was upon him. At the United Nations, world leaders played by parish finance committee volunteers, sat behind cafeteria tables draped with the flags of many nations. They debated and shouted at each other, threatening to go to all out war. That's when the Archbishop of County Mayo, played by Father Maligan, appeared in long flowing vestments and the tall hat and shepherd's cane.

The piano player trembled some upstart Irish chords.

"Listen up, you birds," Maligan told the UN delegates.

"Out of order. Who is this man?" yelled the delegate from Great Britain.

"You mind your place, England. This is a job for the Irish."

Irish parishioners applauded.

Mimi opened Miss Kleinschmidt's desk drawer, the one on the left where she kept her box of crackers. She took out the crackers and opened the opposite drawer on the right, moved some things around, and put the crackers in there.

"Done, let's go," she said.

"That's it?" Patrick said, "You brought us up here for just that?"

"Yeah, shouldn't we crumble them up all over her desk top at least?" Tony asked.

"No, just moving them is enough," Mimi said. "You'll see."

Patrick and Tony looked at each other. For the first time in a while, Tony could see that Mimi didn't know everything. Patrick seized the moment, hoping to drive a wedge between Tony and Mimi.

"Look, we got into this school your way," Patrick said to Mimi, "but let's get out of it my way."

"OK, what?" she said.

Tony looked at Patrick.

"We need to split up, so we won't all three get caught," Patrick said. He wanted to go with Tony so if they got caught, they could bust loose for the tracks together and run away. But before he could say that, Mimi jumped in.

"You're right," she said, "Me and Tony will go one way and you go the other."

Tony grabbed Mimi's hand as if they were jumping off a river bluff together. "We'll meet at the bridge," Tony said. "Good luck."

"Good luck." Patrick watched Tony and Mimi run out the door. He looked at Miss Kleinschmidt's desk and the empty room and walked out slowly, without a plan.

Father Ernst was lurking in the dark of the first floor hallway behind the statue of St. Joseph. He heard running. Two figures ran past him. He couldn't see their faces, but he knew a third wouldn't be far behind. Then he heard footsteps. He shot his arm out and grabbed the criminal.

Sister Mathilda screamed and started slapping her attacker.

Detective Kurtz, still sitting behind the desk in the investigation room, heard the scream and jumped up. He ran out into the hallway and saw Father Ernst apologizing to Sister Mathilda as she righted her habit. Then she took his arm and he led her into the gym. Detective Kurtz was alone in the dark hallway about to give up.

Way down at the other end, he heard footsteps. A boy came down the steps and stood still facing him, silhouetted by the red Exit sign. Patrick could also see someone silhouetted by the Exit sign at the opposite end of the hallway. Patrick squinted into the distance. Whoever it was seemed to be facing him. Then he could see the shape of his gun holster. He knew who it was. Detective Kurtz began to walk slowly toward Patrick, lessening the distance between them to a hundred feet.

The crowd inside the gym shouted with excitement.

Detective Kurtz walked closer. Patrick stood still. Plenty of time to boogie out the door. But Patrick was thinking. What if he just got caught alone? Was he ready to run away from home alone? Would it be any fun without Tony? He thought and thought and thought, while the black polished shoes of Detective Kurtz got seventy-five feet away, then sixty, then fifty.

"Don't try to run," Detective Kurtz said, his voice calm, soothing. "Just stand still and it will be all right."

Patrick obeyed.

Detective Kurtz was a mere forty feet away, his hand reaching for the handcuffs on his belt. "Just stand still. I'm here to help you."

Patrick closed his eyes and waited.

The gymnasium door between Patrick and Detective Kurtz flung open. With a loud roar, a crowd of parish men carrying Monsignor O'Day burst out. "Call an ambulance," shouted Mickey Riley, the former usher whose confession O'Day had heard earlier in the week. O'Day had attempted a George M. Cohan wall kick during the show, fell, and broke his leg. Patrick opened his eyes. The men holding Monsignor O'Day filled the hallway, and all he could see over the crowd was Detective Kurtz's hat. He turned and ran.

"Don't make a fuss," O'Day said raising his hand to bless the crowd. His black wig fell off and someone bent over to scoop it up as Detective Kurtz tried to push through the mob. But it was too late. The wig was kicked across the floor as the boy in the dark fled the scene. A delegate from the United Nations and several soldiers who had danced with O'Day near the trenches grabbed Detective Kurtz.

"Thank God you're here," the UN delegate said, "You can radio for an ambulance much quicker than the phone."

Detective Kurtz took his walkie-talkie from his belt and radioed the dispatcher.

Patrick found Tony smoking a Camel non-filter at the bridge, but Mimi had already left.

"Where is she?" Patrick asked.

"All I did was try to make out a little," Tony said.

"What did she do?"

"She turned her head and said she likes me, but not like that."

"You never know with girls," Patrick said. They walked along the tracks both missing Mimi, but not willing to admit it. If a freight train had come along good and slow right then, Tony might have agreed to leave town with Patrick. But the tracks were quiet. And they decided maybe they should both get back to their homes and pretend they never went out that night for the sake of an alibi, if they needed one later.

CHAPTER 30

THE LAST WEEK of eighth grade finally arrived. It was Monday morning, and Patrick and Tony walked to school the same way they had for years. It was sunny, hot, and windy. As they approached the building, they looked up at the sets of windows, each representing a classroom they'd done time in as they progressed toward eighth grade. In just five days, the whole experience of being in grade school would end. When the last bell of the last day rang, they would get up from their desks to leave, but try as they might, they couldn't imagine what that moment would feel like. No kid could remember all they'd been through, all the bones of their former selves they had scrambled over in the long climb from grade to grade. Instead of joy and anticipation, there was emptiness, a blank chalkboard, a feeling without a name yet. It was the first tug of the constant uncertainty of the adult world, of not being told exactly what to do, of not having the school building looming over them anymore telling them who they are—gradeschoolers.

The bell rang. Patrick and Tony slunk into the classroom where they'd hidden behind the bookshelf Saturday night. It was bright with sunlight and glaring overhead lights. Most of the students were already in their desks. Miss Kleinschmidt was seated behind hers. She looked up at them, sniffed, and looked back down at some paperwork. They took their seats. Mimi's desk was empty.

"Today in history, May, 21, 1864. The Battle of Spotsylvania ended with 32,000 causalities."

Mimi was home sick. She got a chill Saturday night and by Sunday night had a runny nose, cough, and low-grade fever. Although she was feeling better by Monday morning, when her mom told her to stay home and rest, she was relieved. The pressure of the past week had left her exhausted. She lay on her back listening to the birds outside and a passing train and dozed off smiling at the thought of Miss Kleinschmidt noticing her crackers missing.

"Well, it's the last week," Miss Kleinschmidt told the class, "but that doesn't mean we're going to get lazy or coast. Who can name the planets?"

Several hands went up. Miss Kleinschmidt looked around. She noticed Tony's hand was not up.

"Mister Vivamano," she said turning toward him, "stand up."

Tony got up.

"Yes, ma'am."

"Mister Vivamano, I believe you and I have had this discussion before about the importance of knowing more than just that you are alive on planet Earth when you go to … where is it?"

"St. Aloysius."

"That's right. I forgot. But a proper freshman at St. Aloysius should know his planets. Don't you agree?"

"I guess so, ma'am," Tony said softly.

"You guess so? Can you name the planets for us this morning?"

Tony rubbed his face with his hands. "Maybe."

Patrick watched. Everyone watched, hoping that Tony could do it. If he could, Miss Kleinschmidt might go easy on the whole class, maybe for the rest of the day. Nine planets hanging in space, somewhere beyond the school roof, had to be named in the correct order, or else she would explode.

"Stand up straight," she told him.

He threw back his shoulders and held his hands in together in front like he was going to communion.

"We're waiting," she said.

Tony closed his eyes to imagine the center of the sun, which he remembered was twenty-seven million degrees hot. Moving away from the sun's core into space he began to see the planets lined up as best he could.

His lips parted. "The first one, closest to the sun is Mercury."

"That's easy enough, go on."

"The second one is Venus."

"I know you know the next one, it's your favorite."

"Earth."

Miss Kleinschmidt waited, knowing Tony would falter next and name the moon. She was poised to lash out at him for being a failure in planetary science. But Tony surprised everyone.

"Mars."

The students began to wriggle in their desks, moving their lips silently to name the next planet, hoping Tony knew too.

"Jupiter."

The class erupted in cheers.

"Silence! This isn't a hockey game," Miss Kleinschmidt said scowling at the class. Everyone put their hands down and she turned back to Tony. "Don't stop. If you really know your planets, don't name them in dribs and drabs, rattle them off!"

"Saturn, Uranus, Neptune and Pluto."

The room was silent. Miss Kleinschmidt was disappointed, but also proud of herself that she had finally taught Tony to learn the facts. "OK, OK, you can sit down now, Mister Vivamano. Don't stand their gloating over something everyone with any sense knows. You got it right this time. Now, let's all get out our science books and I want you to review the Milky Way for the final test."

Tony sat down and everyone shot him approving glances. They got out their science books, knowing it was going to be a quiet morning, because Tony had robbed Miss Kleinschmidt of her chance to get mad. She sat down at her desk and opened her desk drawer to have a cracker.

They were gone.

"Who took them?" she said.

Everyone looked up.

Miss Kleinschmidt reviewed her movements of the morning to visualize when the desk had been unguarded—and who was in the room and who wasn't. She looked at Tony and Patrick, but remembered they had only arrived after the bell when she was at her desk. She looked for Mimi, but her desk was empty. She throttled back her chair and stood up.

"I want to know who took them! Who took them?"

Sarah Jebbs, a girl who never did anything wrong, raised her hand.

"Was it you?" Miss Kleinschmidt thundered.

"Why, no, I mean, I was only raising my hand to ask what somebody took."

"So, you don't know?" She paced back and forth studying faces. "Nobody knows? You expect me to think that something like this could just happen, after what already happened with the snow globe? Well, we'll just see about this." She pointed at Patrick and shouted. "You! Mr. Cantwell, go downstairs right now and ask Sister Helen, Detective Kurtz, and Father Ernst to come up here right away."

Patrick leaped up. "Yes, ma'am. What should I tell them?"

"Tell them it's an emergency."

"Yes, ma'am." He ran out the door and down the stairs.

"And the rest of you, empty out your desks. I want the complete contents of your desks on your desktops right now."

Everyone obeyed. Textbooks thudded on desktops, followed by notebooks and scraps of paper. No one knew what it was about—no one except Tony. A slight smirk crossed his face and Miss Kleinschmidt spotted it.

"Vivamano!" she yelled, pointing a boney finger at his face, "What makes you so happy?"

"Me? I'm just happy I know the planets."

Miss Kleinschmidt hurried back to Patrick's desk, emptying it out herself. His book on Dillinger came out last and she threw it on the floor. Then she hurried toward the back of the room, keeping one eye on the students, while she peeked in the cloakroom. It was such a warm day no one brought coats to hide the crackers in. Hurrying to solve the case, she went over to the bookcase, flinging books on the floor to see if the crackers were hidden behind them. She started calling out the title of books as she threw them.

"Moby Dick, Treasure Island, How to Win Friends and Influence People …"

The principal and Detective Kurtz and Father Ernst ran in followed by Patrick. They all stopped by the door and saw Miss Kleinschmidt panting by a pile of books on the floor.

"Good Lord, Miss Kleinschmidt, are you all right?" Sister Helen asked.

Nodding yes, and holding her index finger in the air, Miss Kleinschmidt caught her breath and hurried over to her desk.

"What is it?" the principal asked. "Is there a medical emergency?"

Miss Kleinschmidt shook her head no. Sister Helen, Father Ernst, and Detective Kurtz all looked at each other wondering what was wrong.

"It's this!" she said pulling out her empty desk drawer and holding it up for all to see. "They've stolen my crackers."

All the students looked at the principal and the investigators to see what they would do.

"They've stolen your crackers?" the principal repeated, hoping she had heard it wrong.

Miss Kleinschmidt nodded, still a little winded. "That's right. I bought a full box just the other day. It must've happened this morning. I told them to empty out their desks for the search." Her eyes were wide open like a fisherman with a big one the line. "Now, if you'll help with the search—" She started coughing badly and made a dramatic gulp to get the phlegm back down.

"You need some water. Come with me," Sister Helen said.

Miss Kleinschmidt started hacking up even more mucus and followed the principal out the door. Father Ernst walked behind the children along the back of the room. He could see their desktops stacked with books and empty compartments below their seats. "Children, what do we know about this?"

They all turned around shaking their heads and saying "nothing."

Father Ernst looked at Detective Kurtz. Kurtz walked up to Miss Kleinschmidt's desk and sat behind it. All the kids looked at him. He opened the middle drawer, full of pens and pencils and charts. Closing that, he opened the bottom right drawer and saw the box of crackers. He looked up at Father Ernst. Then he pulled out the Saltine Jumbo Size box and put it on Miss Kleinschmidt's desk.

He looked around the room to see who looked guilty. Tony and Patrick looked away when his eyes met theirs. Their guilt could be related to the snow globe or the crackers, or both. He didn't know. He noticed Mimi's desk was empty.

Detective Kurtz got up and walked out of the room without saying anything. That was the scary part for Patrick and Tony. What was Kurtz thinking? Father Ernst followed him out and shut the door. All the kids started laughing and talking. Patrick and Tony didn't tell anyone what they knew. It was the best morning they had ever had in eighth grade. They only wished Mimi had been there to enjoy it. She was probably at home picturing the whole thing unfold just the way she planned it. That Mimi was a genius. She was probably laughing her guts out having a great time.

Mimi was home alone vomiting into the toilet.

CHAPTER 31

MIMI WAS PREGNANT. Or so she feared. How could this be? She had only had sex once—without planning to—but she knew that was all it took. It had been Easter break when the ground on the golf course was still warm at night and Skip had told her he loved her. They were kissing and grabbing and rolling in the grass and just kept going. That stupid, damned Skip, that stupid, damned golf course, that stupid, damned thing, love. For Mimi, it was a one-time sin she was willing to forgive him for, and avoid again, because she had loved him, too. She had loved him enough to try to switch high schools and be with him. Now, after vomiting, she had puked out every last chunk and morsel of feeling she once had for Skip. She flushed the toilet.

Mimi took off her clothes to take a shower and turned to look at herself in the mirror. Her breasts looked bigger than the day before. She held them in her hands for size and winced. It was the tenderness that sent her running naked across the hall to her room to find the *Seventeen* magazine on the floor, the issue with the article about pregnancy that she had read once and cast aside.

She picked up the magazine, sat on her bed, and read the whole article again.

"Maybe it's just a cold," she said aloud.

Then she read the list of symptoms again and cried.

She hid the magazine under her bed and got under the covers and put a pillow over her head against the sunlight. Sleep came, but it was a jittery sleep. She wished she had never met Skip, never dreamed of going to public school with him. She wished she were like all the other kids, graduating in a few days with nothing but a carefree summer ahead. She wished the hand grenade had worked.

CHAPTER 32

THE REST OF THE MORNING was tense. First the principal came in and told the class in her soft, authoritative voice that they should all pray for Miss Kleinschmidt, and be nice to her and make the rest of the school year go smoothly, because she was "under a tremendous strain". No one felt moved to pray for her. She had only gotten what she deserved after months of cruelty. Then the principal ordered the students to put away all their textbooks, and pick up the ones on the floor to put back in the bookcase. After the classroom was tidy, she left, and Miss Kleinschmidt returned.

"Class, I have something to tell you," she said limping up to her desk.

She sat down and apologized for getting mad. She said that teachers give up their whole lives to help children become adults and she only got mad because she cared so much about their future. Nobody believed that, but she seemed to believe it. After a few more stories about her walking to school in the snow as a girl and studying hard to get ahead, she looked at the clock and told them they could all go outside and have an extra recess today, because the school year was almost over.

"Thanks, Miss Kleinschmidt," Sarah Jibbs said.

She smiled at Sarah and at a few other students who also seemed appreciative. Tony was heading toward the door when he heard her call her name.

"Mister Vivamano?"

He stopped and turned around. "Me?"

"Yes, you. Go see Father Ernst and Detective Kurtz. I understand they have something for you."

Tony looked at Patrick, who raised his eyebrows to say he didn't know what that could be.

"Yes, ma'am," Tony said.

CHAPTER 33

THE MOST FUN Tony and Patrick ever had was the night they slept out in a tent in Tony's backyard with their fishing poles and tackle boxes ready by their bikes to go fishing before sunup at Holy Footsteps Academy. The pond at Holy Footsteps was renowned for catfish as big as footballs, along with leagues of bluegill, frogs, and snapping turtles. It was late in the summer before fifth grade. Tony's family had just moved into the parish, and when he met Patrick, they liked each other right away. They had met on the altar boy's serving team, but hadn't been fired yet.

"Time to get up," Tony said.

A little before five o'clock in the morning, they rose out of the tent, put on their tennis shoes, ate beef jerky, and drank ice water from an army canteen. They rode their bikes to the pond—the same pond where later they would wait when Mimi sneaked into Holy Footsteps. Only this time, it was just the two of them, and the water was stirring with promise of dawn. They baited their hooks and cast out with a plop. Catfish and blue gill were biting. Cars went by on the road, the cars of parents who had to go to work, even though it was summer. Some looked over at the boys wishing they were young.

By noon they had a stringer of catfish, which they draped between the handlebars of Patrick's bike. On the way home, a carload of teenaged boys rode past them. A guy leaned out the window and threw a Styrofoam to-go cup of piping hot Kentucky Fried Chicken gravy on Patrick. It exploded on the right side of his face and he crashed his bike. Catfish skidded on the asphalt, wide-eyed, with gills still moving. He couldn't ride, so Tony let him sit on his seat while he pedaled home. After that, Patrick loved Tony. When Patrick later got them fired as altar boys, they both loved each other.

"Have a seat Mr. Vivamano," Detective Kurtz said, as Tony entered the interrogation room.

He sat down and looked around. This time the overhead lights were on, no spot light in the face. Father Ernst was sitting on the sofa bench again with a file folder in his hand. It was the Tony Vivamano file.

"Where were you Saturday night?" Detective Kurtz asked.

Tony thought of climbing in the bathroom window, running through the school, and hiding in Miss Kleinschmidt's class. "Me? I was at home, I think. Yeah, I was watching TV."

"What was on?"

Tony tried to remember the Saturday night shows. "I watch TV a lot, probably too much, so let me think. This Saturday, it was probably *Love, American Style*."

"That's on Friday nights, isn't it?" Detective Kurtz said looking over at Father Ernst.

"I don't know. I've never seen it."

"Yeah, you're right," Tony said, "I got mixed up. Saturday night it was *Mary Tyler Moore* and then *The Bob Newhart Show*."

"What happened on the Mary Tyler Moore show?"

Tony knew he couldn't make up something specific, so he kept it vague. "Well, this week's show began with her throwing her hat up in the air and catching it."

"She does that every show," Detective Kurtz said. "Can you remember anything about the plot?"

"Sure, it was about Mary working in a newsroom with her boss, Mr. Grant. He yelled at her some and then this other guy, the anchorman Ted Baxter, he kinda walked around saying some stupid things." Tony fake laughed like it was a really good show. "That Ted."

"Look, as you know, some kids busted into the school over the weekend," Detective Kurtz said, "Just tell us what you stole and it will go a lot easier on you later."

Tony shook his head innocently and shrugged. "I'm sorry, I don't know anything about that. This is the first I've heard. That's terrible."

Detective Kurtz knew he was lying, but that was OK. He had Tony nervous now and that was part of the interrogation strategy. "You're pretty close friends with Patrick Cantwell aren't you?"

Tony treaded carefully. "Oh, he's a good guy. We hang out some."

Father Ernst reached out with a gentle gesture to gain Tony's confidence. "Tony? May I call you Tony?"

He nodded OK.

"Tony, I understand from what Patrick told us that you and he used to be altar boys together."

Tony saw the image of Father Maligan swinging open the Mens room door, as Patrick fake glugged the wine. "Yes, that's right. We served together."

"Are you no longer an altar boy?" Father Ernst asked.

"No."

"Tell me, how was it that you stopped serving Mass?"

Tony knew that they knew something, so he played a trick on them. He told them the truth. Hell, he thought, he was already fired. They couldn't fire him twice. "Well, the truth is, Father, I'm ashamed to admit it, but Father Maligan caught me one day with Patrick, when I was drinking the wine."

Father Ernst opened his file and glanced at his notes from his conversation with Father Maligan. "*You* were drinking the wine?"

"Yeah, that's right."

"I had understood it was Patrick who was drinking the wine."

"Is that what you've got," Tony said looking at the file upside down, "Well, it was so long ago, I can't remember everything. He might've been thirsty, too."

Detective Kurtz moved in for the kill. "I can tell you like this Patrick a lot."

Tony didn't answer him. He watched Detective Kurtz and waited.

"You cover for him on the wine story. Maybe you're covering for him on a lot of other things. Are you sure about this guy Patrick, that he's really your friend?"

Tony nodded.

Detective Kurtz looked over at Father Ernst who opened the file and held up the photograph he had taken of Patrick kissing Mimi.

The room was quiet. Tony was cut in half. His feet started pumping with blood ready to run a thousand miles.

"Don't be so quiet, kid," Detective Ernst said. "Tell us what you think of this Patrick guy now. I mean, doesn't he know that you love Mimi? If you told us you loved her, you must've told him. And here he is stealing a kiss from her when you're not looking. Is he you're friend now? Do you really want to cover for a guy like that and get yourself in deeper shit?"

Tony thought of his dad's copy of the book *The Godfather*, how when a guy was getting grilled the only thing to do was not crack, not say anything, even right up to the point of getting shot.

Detective Kurtz stood up and shouted. "SAY SOMETHING, KID, OR YOU AND PATRICK AND MIMI WILL ALL BE IN THE SAME SHIT TOGETHER, ONLY PATRICK'LL BE KISSING MIMI AND YOU'LL BE LEFT WITH NOTHING BUT THE SHIT."

Tony took a very dignified breath and flexed his eyebrows like a man of many romances. "Did I say I loved Mimi? I can't remember. I've been in love before, and I'll be in love again. Let's not get all upset about it."

Detective Kurtz sat down and smiled. "I'm not upset," he said softly, "We're just both trying to help you. Right, Father?"

Tony looked over at Father Ernst who closed the file. "That's right. We just want you to consider telling the truth, if there's anything you haven't told us. Think about it now, and thank you for your time."

"You're welcome," Tony said. He stood up like a man whose horse had just won, then he closed the door, walked down the hallway alone, and wept.

CHAPTER 34

PRESIDENT NIXON BOWLED in his underwear on sublevel sixteen of the White House basement. Riding the elevator down to find him, Secretary of State Henry Kissinger, wearing a dark suit, which he buttoned against the chill of the room, entered the super secret bowling alley designed to survive a direct nuclear blast. Nixon had cranked up the air conditioner all the way and was listening to an Elvis Presley record playing loudly.

"Mr. President, it's freezing down here," Kissinger said.

Nixon nodded, his face flinty with concentration, as he laid down another ball that scorched toward a strike.

"Very good, sir," Kissinger said as the pins scattered and fell.

"Henry, I've been thinking," the president said, standing with his chest out and hands on his hips.

"Yes?"

"This Watergate stuff is trivial."

Elvis started singing "Love Me Tender."

"But Mr. President, John Dean is scheduled to testify. What if he links you to the cover-up?"

The automatic pinsetter rose up, leaving another batch of pins ready for the next ball. The president put some talcum powder on his hands, and patted the extra on his chest. "You ever think about destiny, Henry?"

"Not extensively, sir. I believe that each of us—"

"Destiny," Nixon said grabbing a fresh ball, "is the idea that this ball, in the hands of the right bowler, is going to accomplish something great."

"That's true to a point, sir, but there are variables."

Nixon wound up, but held the ball against his chest and turned to Kissinger.

"Variables exist, but in the larger scheme of things, they must yield to the flow of history, the flow of destiny."

Kissinger got out a piece of paper from the breast pocket of his suit coat. "I have the draft of the statement on the Watergate situation for your approval."

Nixon took one hand off the bowling ball to wave off the document. "Now, I want to make this crystal clear. Think about this, Henry."

"Yes, sir?"

"God wouldn't have let me win re-election just to blow me out of the water with this Watergate trivia. I still feel I'm destined for something great."

"Yes, of course, but we must make sure the statement answers all the concerns of the American—"

"The American public? Hell, it was a landslide. The people have spoken."

Kissinger paused. "Yes, sir, they have. But the Senate Watergate Committee—"

"Nobody in Boise cares about that."

"Perhaps not yet, but they might. Is there anything more you want to say in the statement, other than what we discussed at the pool?" Kissinger asked.

"I don't know ... just deny any involvement in the cover-up and throw in a lot of national security shit to distract them."

Kissinger got out his pen. "National security stuff?"

"You know, mention the Pentagon Papers and say we're damned concerned American lives are in danger. Brave young men in harm's way because of these criminal leaks. Tell them we were doing a lot of wiretapping and intelligence for national security purposes."

"I see," Kissinger said taking notes.

"Do that and this Watergate break-in will seem like a trivial side show. The American people ... they'll give me the benefit of the doubt."

"OK."

"Can you do it, Henry, I mean can you get right on it?"

Kissinger looked at his watch. "I'll have to break a ... an appointment."

Nixon took his stance and concentrated on the pins. "Henry, even if you have to miss a date, God's will be done."

"Yes, Mister President."

Nixon skipped down the alley, flinging the ball like an atomic bomb aimed right at *The Washington Post*. It shot down the lane and knocked over all but two pins.

"Damn, it's Woodward and Bernstein again," Nixon mumbled.

"Pardon me, sir?"

"Nothing, I'll take care of these last two. You just put together that statement and the rest we'll leave up to destiny."

"Yes, sir." Kissinger left to prepare the president's first official statement on Watergate for release the next day. Nixon hurled another ball down the lane toward the last two pins.

CHAPTER 35

PATRICK SPENT RECESS playing horse at the basketball net with a third grader. He had never met the kid, but wanted to have something to do in a corner of the playground where he could spot Tony right away when he came out from his interrogation. Patrick was terrible at basketball. The suspense of the investigation and wondering what Tony was saying made him miss even more shots. The third grader was an expert. He could dribble in elaborate figure eight patterns and then make perfect layups that Patrick had to duplicate to keep up. "You lose again," the kid said.

"Maybe I'm letting you win," Patrick said double-dribbling.

"I don't think so. You wanna play for money?"

"No thanks, I'm just waiting for somebody to come out."

"You in that class that put the snow globe up there in Mary's hand?"

Patrick stopped dribbling and looked at him. "How'd you know about that?"

"Everybody in the whole school knows. Whoever did that is going to hell. Was it you?"

Patrick took a shot at the basket and missed.

After recess, Patrick filed inside the school, walking up the same old steps to the top floor and into Miss Kleinschmidt's class. She was seated behind her desk, and Tony was already at his desk with his back to the students returning from recess. Patrick wanted to hear all the news on how the interrogation went, but Tony never looked back, not even for a wink. Something was up.

Father Ernst walked in. He was by himself. All the students tensed up, wondering who would be called for more questioning. Patrick slouched down a little.

Miss Kleinschmidt saw him and stood up.

"Today for religion I thought it might be helpful if Father Ernst gave you all a little lesson." She nodded to him and took her pack of cigarettes and walked out to go to the teacher's lounge.

Father Ernst sat on the front edge of her desk with his legs stretched out and crossed at the ankles. Everyone waited. Tony kept his head down. Patrick began to doodle a picture of a freight train going across a long, flat farm field with hay bails and a barn nearby. It was the kind of barn he and Tony would soon be sleeping in on their escape from the future.

"I was thinking on this lovely May day how the Blessed Mother has appeared to children, children just like you, to reveal some special message." Patrick relaxed a little. At least he wasn't talking about the investigation. Obviously, Father Ernst was trying to make them all feel guilty again for not telling the truth about whoever put the snow globe in Mary's hand. He talked about shepherd children and little girls going about their business when suddenly Mary would appear in bright clothing telling them how she was praying for their village and something bad was going to happen if they didn't get right.

"In France, a little town called La Salette," Father Ernst said, "two children named Melanie and Max were watching after some cattle in the hills when a ball of light appeared and it opened up and there she was, sitting with her face in her hands crying."

Patrick looked over at Tony, who still had his head down. Somehow, they had really got to him. If only Mimi were here, she would cheer him up. Patrick looked over at Mimi's empty desk and wondered what she was doing right now. Mimi was probably watching TV, laughing at some show, and having a great time after faking a sick day to get out of the investigation. That Mimi had an easy life. She even got to miss this boring lecture.

"Our Blessed Mother told them she was holding onto her son's arm and praying for their village to stop being bad. And do you know what they were doing?"

No one knew. No one moved.

"They were doing the same things we all do," Father Ernst said, "We're no better. The men were cursing when they pushed their heavy carts, and only a few old ladies in the village went to Mass on Sunday. Everyone else mocked religion. They worked on Sunday like it was another day. She warned them that unless people changed, bad things would happen to the village. Crops would fail. People would go hungry. She told them to warn the villagers to change before it was too late."

Jimmy Purvis raised his hand.

"Yes?" Father Ernst said.

As one of the Gang of Five who had run away in fifth grade, Jimmy was a tough customer. He wasn't sold on the story. "That's a nice story, Father, but did they get any evidence?"

"Evidence?"

"You know, a photograph. I thought maybe, if these two kids really saw something, they'd run home and get a Kodak to take some snapshots."

"Oh, no, this was 1846. Cameras weren't even invented."

"I see." Jimmy nodded his head and didn't say any more. He looked at his watch.

Father Ernst cleared his throat and walked around a bit, holding his chin in his hand. Then he turned to the class. "No one can prove these things, but to me, they have the melody of truth. It's a proof you can hear with your heart. Does that make sense?"

No one said anything. It was almost time for lunch and stomachs were empty.

"Well, think about what happened to Melanie and Max," Father Ernst said. "Think about what they would tell you if they were your friends here at school and they knew about what someone did to the statue in this parish of the same Blessed Mary who appeared to them with such concern for their souls, and the souls of their whole village."

Father Ernst walked out. It was time for lunch. But Miss Kleinschmidt wasn't there to dismiss them. With just a few days left under her authority, some of students got up on their own, retrieved their lunch bags from the cloak room, and headed out the door to walk down to the cafeteria. Others followed. The whole class emptied out like a graduation, because it was time and they were hungry.

CHAPTER 36

A SINGLE FAT RAINDROP fell on the cheek of the unchanging, ever motionless gold statute of Mary on the church roof. Then another. And another. Tony and Patrick's class was sitting down to lunch in the basement cafeteria when the tornado siren sounded in the distance. It was a low, howling note that rose up the scale to a solid wail. Everyone heard it.

"Tony," Patrick whispered sitting next to him, "You OK? What happened?"

Tony refused to speak. He ate his cold meatball sandwich and stared forward. Outside the school, the gusting wind bent trees, whipping leaves across the playground. First graders dropped kick balls and sprinted through the cold rain for the door. Mothers' Club volunteers standing at the door waved them in. Sister Mathilda was pacing back and forth in her harness attached to the clothesline—with one corner of her black eye patches unpeeled—keeping an eye on the little children before she would take shelter herself.

Sister Helen turned on the microphone in her office and every speaker in every classroom turned on with a red blinking light.

"Attention everyone, this is the principal," she said, "This is not a drill. The National Weather Service has issued a tornado warning for St. Louis County. Everyone file calmly out of your classrooms and walk slowly down to the cafeteria."

The fear of death fell on the school. Children seeing the sideways rain and trembling tree branches through the windows got up from their desks to run for the basement. Lightening flashed. The school lights flickered out. There was stumbling and screaming in the hallways.

Sister Mathilda unhooked her harness from the clothesline to go inside. Just a few more days and her escape would be a matter of parish gossip: *So she really did it? She was smarter than we thought. Yes sir, they'd say, old Sister Mathilda was too smart to be forced into some retirement home. We had her all wrong.*

"Help!" It was a child's voice.

Sister Mathilda ripped her eye patch off and before she could put it in her pocket, the wind tore it from her fingers. It skittered across the playground.

"Help me."

She looked around. The voice sounded like it was coming from over near her Cutlass. She hurried over to find a first grade boy hiding alone between the parked cars. She grabbed him by the arm. "Get up, son."

She tried to pull him up, but he was scared limp. So she reached in her pocket for her rosary pouch, unzipped it, and drew the Cutlass key out like a sword. Opening the door with rain blasting her face, she picked up the boy and tossed him in like a load of laundry. Then she got in and slammed the door. Hail the size of mothballs pounded the car and bounced across the parking lot. The wind picked up. The Cutlass rocked. "Buckle up," she yelled. He couldn't even do that, so she clicked him in tight.

Inside, hundreds of students streamed down the steps into the cafeteria. In an effort to maintain calm, the fourth grade music teacher, Miss Olgers, started strumming "My Favorite Things" on her guitar. But a sudden surge of sixth graders knocked her over and the guitar was crushed underfoot.

"Everyone stay calm," the principal called out through a bullhorn. "We're in the safest place possible."

Just then a kitchen fire erupted, as a cook watching the chaos had neglected a pan of breaded fish sticks frying in lard on the gas stove. The flames danced over the fish and into the air four feet above the frying pan. A quick thinking cashier in charge of milk and pretzel stick sales turned off the burner and poured chocolate milk on the conflagration. The dying fire hissed and cursed and filled the cafeteria with a sickly, burnt chocolate smell.

Patrick got under the cafeteria table facing Tony and put his hands on Tony's shoulders.

"Tony, please tell me. What happened? What did they say to you?"

Tony told him about the photograph, the one of Patrick kissing Mimi. "I won't get in the way," Tony said. "But I can't be your friend anymore."

Patrick took his hands off Tony's shoulders, and Tony scooted away and disappeared into the crowd.

The tornado cut across the nunnery yard and pushed over a row of cars. The Cutlass flipped upside down. Sister Mathilda and the boy hung tight in their seat belts.

"It's all my fault," she told the boy.

The Cutlass rolled sideways, like a Hot Wheels car, turning over twelve times before it bounced off the fence down by the priest's house and came to a stop on all four tires.

"Are you all right?" Sister Mathilda asked the boy.

"I think I wet my pants."

The new car smell was gone forever. The Cutlass was mangled and dented, the roof flattened, the windows cracked—it was no longer road worthy.

Just as fast as it struck, the tornado moved on. The playground was now bright with sunlight. Sister Mathilda creaked open her door. It was fifteen degrees cooler. Drenched tree branches drooping over the playground fence dripped water into the glare of puddles.

"C'mon, let's go." She unbuckled the boy and they both got out. His hair was flecked with glass crumbs. She brushed them out. They looked at the school and the church and the gold statue on the roof. Mary gleamed bright in the sun. Everything was OK. Sister Mathilda knelt on the blacktop to give thanks. It was her first non-complaining prayer in a long time. Waking up from a nap, Father Maligan flung open his bedroom window to survey the aftermath.

"Hey, Sister Mathilda, whose car is that? Is there a storm coming? You need some help finding your way?"

She waved no thanks to him and mumbled to herself as she got up. "I can see just fine."

CHAPTER 37

AFTER THE STORM, the lights came back on in the school and the students walked back upstairs to their desks. Only the boy who took the carnival ride of death in the Cutlass got to go home early, and that was because he had wet his pants. A tow truck came and hauled away Sister Mathilda's wrecked escape car to take it to the auto graveyard. She went into the church to pray some more. Father Ernst and Detective Kurtz suspended their investigation for the rest of the day, sparing Patrick the follow up interrogation he dreaded was coming. They wanted him to dread it.

Same thing the next day. Patrick sat in his desk waiting to be summoned, taking occasional glances at Tony who was still not talking to him. Not calling Patrick in for more questions was Detective Kurtz's idea. He knew it would make Tony think Patrick was no longer a suspect, that they'd pinned the caper on Tony.

With the door to their interrogation room shut all day long, Father Ernst and Detective Kurtz reviewed the case they had only three days left to solve. Kurtz set up an easel board and used a black marker to draw diagrams of a pyramid with Patrick, Tony, and Mimi at the top. It was Mimi, they theorized, who was at the very top—and it was Mimi they wanted to interview again. But her desk was empty for a second straight day.

Home with a low-grade fever and a glass of Alka-Seltzer, Mimi lay in bed, but couldn't fall asleep because there was a piano tuner downstairs. He would hit a note over and over, tightening a wrench on a bolt attached to a wire to get the note in tune. Mimi got out of bed and drifted out in her back yard in her pajamas, bathrobe, and slippers. It was sunny and mild, the day after the big storm. She could still hear the piano tuner, so she walked along engrossed in her real problem—how to handle the possibility she was pregnant. This fear pressed on her chest like a thousand-pound piano. She had told no one. *How could she?* Lost in thought, she walked onto the golf course, oblivious to the fallen tree limbs from the storm and the businessmen in the distance hitting balls.

"Four!" a golfer yelled.

Mimi walked on with her hands held behind her back reviewing all her troubles as a golf ball thumped in the wet grass at her side. She picked it up with a vacant look on her face and wandered down the fairway, playing catch with it lightly while she concentrated.

"Just three days to graduation," she thought. "Just three days to graduation."

Her mind stretched like a piano wire wrenched tighter and tighter ready to snap. The note kept plinking in her head while she walked. *Plink, plink, plink, plink, plink …*

Just three more days. Just three more days.

Then the note stopped.

Her mind was in tune.

She knew what to do. Pretend she wasn't pregnant. Just fool herself. That's it. Just forget it. Forget it for three more days until school was over. If she were pregnant, she'd find out in the weeks ahead. If she weren't pregnant, it wouldn't do any good to worry about it now. Not now, with the snow globe crisis she had promised to help Tony and Patrick with. They had saved her life from the hand grenade and she had to stick to the plan they made for the next three days. After that—school would be over and she could figure things out. For now, she resolved to play out the lie of not knowing anything about the case, and blaming it on Mary. When the school year was over she would be free to think about her future either at Holy Footsteps or Holy Shit Academy.

An angry golfer on a cart zoomed up alongside her and braked to a stop, skidding in the mud. "Hey young lady, that's my ball," he said.

Mimi blinked and noticed something odd. She was in her bathrobe, holding a golf ball, standing on the golf course talking to a strange man.

The golfer stared at her. "Jesus, Mary, and Joseph, what's wrong with you?"

Mimi handed him the ball, apologized, and coughed a little into her hand. "I'm sorry, sir, I'm home sick today."

"Maybe sick in the head."

Mimi burst out laughing. It was the best she'd felt in two days. Her face got red coughing as she bent over shaking with laughter.

The golfer looked warily at her and got back on his cart and drove away.

Mimi tightened her bathrobe belt and fixed her hair. She turned to walk back home and decided if the investigators at school would ask her anymore questions, she should act a little sick in the head, so they, too, would want to drive off and leave her alone with her troubles.

Chapter 38

THE NEXT MORNING the bell rang and everyone sat down. Tony and Patrick had walked to school separately. Tony was sulking. Patrick was depressed. It was sunny out and the windows were open, letting in some air. Miss Kleinschmidt took role and noted that Mimi's desk was still empty. She stood to announce her Today in History headline. "Class, it's May 23rd, and on this day in 1430, Joan of Arc was captured by the British," she said. "She would soon face trial and be burned alive at the stake."

Mimi walked in.

Everyone watched her moving slowly to her desk. She looked a little pale. For breakfast she had eaten two bites of a blueberry Pop-Tart and a half a glass of Slim Fast chocolate shake because the sight of her brother's Fruit Loops turning the milk pink made her want to barf.

"Miss Maloney, so nice of you to finally join us," Miss Kleinschmidt said. She walked over to Mimi's desk to demand a note from her parents explaining her two-day absence. But before she could say so, Mimi handed her a note her mother had written.

> *Dear Miss Kleinschmidt,*
> *Please excuse Mimi for missing two days school this week. She apparently had some virus, but she's feeling well enough to return.*
> *Mrs. Maloney*

Miss Kleinschmidt sniffed and took a step back. "Well, I hope you aren't going to get the rest of us good and sick now. Are you feeling well enough to be breathing on us?"

Mimi nodded yes.

Miss Kleinschmidt turned to go back to her desk, and Mimi turned around to say something to Tony. His head was down.

"Hi, Tony," she whispered.

Tony, nodded, but kept his eyes on the wood grain of his desk.

"I'm looking forward to the graduation dance with you," she whispered.

Tony looked up. "You are?"

Mimi nodded yes and turned back around facing the front of the class. Tony could smell the shampoo fragrance from her hair. "The Stars and Stripes Forever" played in Tony's brain. He sat up straight and smiled.

There was a knock at the door.

Everyone turned to look. It was Detective Kurtz. His blue shirt, shiny badge, and weapons belt were in perfect order. This was going to be a big day for Detective Kurtz. He was ready to finally solve the case. Patrick closed his book on Dillinger and tensed his legs to get up for his interrogation.

"Mimi Maloney," Detective Kurtz called out.

Patrick's legs relaxed.

Mimi stood up.

"Could you please come with me?" Detective Kurtz asked.

She walked around the rows of desks, without much spring in her step.

"So, I hear you've been sick," Detective Kurtz said as they walked down the steps.

Mimi worked up a cough and covered her mouth with her hand. "Oh, yes, I hope you don't catch it. I'm still contagious."

Detective Kurtz deflected her possible attempt to discourage a full session of questioning. "Don't worry about me, Miss Maloney. I never get sick."

At the bottom of the steps Mimi spotted the girls' room. "You mind if I use the bathroom real quick?"

"OK, but don't take all morning in there."

"Yes, sir." She gave him a fake courtesy and ducked in the bathroom. The door closed behind her. She stood in front of the mirror and messed up her hair to look a little deranged. Then she practiced making strange eyes in the mirror and took some deep breaths to look like the Hunch Back of Notre

Dame. The toilet flushed and a second grade girl came out and looked at Mimi. Mimi ran some water and pretended to be just washing her hands.

"You're too big to be in here," the second grade girl said, noticing how Mimi had to lean down to reach the sink.

Mimi smiled at her and kept washing her hands. "You're right, I'm too old for this shit."

When the girl left, Mimi reached in her pocket and pulled out her secret weapon. It was a two-tablet packet of Alka-Seltzer. Tearing the foil wrapper, she took out an Alka-Seltzer tablet and crushed it into little pieces. Then she hid the pieces in a paper towel and tucked the paper towel in her pocket. Her plan was to fake some coughing later, and then bring the paper towel to her mouth to get the Alka-Seltzer pieces in her mouth. That way, her mouth would foam up and she could convince the investigators that she was nuts.

"You OK in there?" Detective Kurtz said knocking outside the door.

Mimi scurried into the stall to flush the toilet to make it sound official.

"Coming."

CHAPTER 39

MIMI WALKED INTO the interrogation room. Detective Kurtz shut the door behind her and sat down behind the desk. Father Ernst was there, like before, sitting on the bench cushion. The room was bright from the overhead lights and the desk lamp shining down on a list of class names. She took her seat, feeling a little weak and warm, but ready to put on a show.

"So, tell me," Detective Kurtz began, "How do you spell meticulous?"

Mimi blinked. The question suggested Detective Kurtz had dove deeper into her grade school file than she had anticipated. But there seemed no harm in playing along for now, even if he knew about her fainting over the word in the fifth grade spelling bee.

"M-e-t-i-c-u-l-o-u-s," she said.

"Very good," Detective Kurtz said smiling. "I was curious after reading in your file about the spelling bee if you remember the word."

"You always remember the word that got you," Mimi said.

Father Ernst said nothing, watching the questions and answers like a ping-pong match.

"I know exactly what you mean," Detective Kurtz said, faking a friendly tone. "It's like police work. You always remember the case you couldn't solve. I also imagine that when a word like 'meticulous' stumps a spelling bee contestant, that she would learn and never forget the meaning of that word."

Mimi nodded. "I suppose so."

"You seem, for instance, to be a very meticulous girl."

"Oh?"

"Why, yes, a girl capable of handling a large project that requires attention to detail, strategy … intelligence."

"I don't know. My grades are average."

"Grades don't always tell the story of the real person and how meticulous she is inside, now do they?"

Mimi shrugged. "What's all this got to do with anything?"

Father Ernst looked over at Detective Kurtz, wondering how he would move onto the next level, or if he had the proper footing to make the climb.

Detective Kurtz got out the envelope containing the fake letter from Holy Footsteps Academy, the one saying the school looked forward to Mimi coming there in the fall.

"Your mother was kind enough to lend me this letter," Detective Kurtz said running his fingertips over the address and postage stamp with the fake cancellation. "I don't know if you've seen it."

Mimi coughed. "We get a lotta letters. Which one is that?"

Detective Kurtz took the letter from the envelope, holding onto the envelope, and handed the letter to Mimi for her to read.

She took it from him and looked it over, acting as if she were reading it for the first time. "Why, this is just another boring letter from the school."

"That's the same reaction I had at first," Detective Kurtz said, "It seems like a standard form letter. A letter from a school where you have been accepted saying they're looking forward to you going there."

Father Ernst posed a question. "Are you looking forward to going to Holy Footsteps?"

"Sure, why not."

"Such a nonchalant answer," Detective Kurtz said, "But this is no ordinary letter. It's a letter that arrived the very day two boys tried to steal the mail from the mailman, or so I thought, until I noticed the postage stamp." He handed the envelope to Father Ernst to examine again. Then Father Ernst gave it to Mimi. She looked at the address, avoiding eye contact with the stamp.

"Look at the stamp," Detective Kurtz said, "It looks canceled, but on closer examination, we see it did not run through an official stamp cancellation machine at the Post Office. Someone drew cancellation lines on it with an ink pen."

"Really?" Mimi said, sitting up a little and acting surprised.

"That's right," Detective Kurtz said, "So I checked with the school, with the principal, Sister Flourie, and she told me that no such letter was sent out or signed by her. It's a complete fake."

"Well, what do you know about that?" Mimi said. She was waiting to see where he would go.

"I didn't know what to think," Detective Kurtz said. "Why would someone go to such great lengths to steal a letter from the mailman that is essentially true? I mean let's look at the facts. You have been accepted. You are expected to go to this school. Right?"

"Yeah." She dazed her eyes and breathed a little heavy like she had practiced in the bathroom.

"So, this letter, which by its fake cancellation we know never went through the mail, must have been composed to replace another fake letter from the school, a letter that arrived despite the efforts of two boys to steal the mail that day."

"How can you prove that? Have you got another fake letter?" Mimi asked. She was feeling better about her case.

"I don't have another fake letter, and I don't need another fake letter, because it's not important."

"It sounds pretty important to me," Mimi said looking over at Father Ernst. When she looked, she noticed her eyes hurt moving to the side, the way they would with a fever.

"What's important is that two boys showed up to steal the letter, boys in their underwear and masks," Detective Kurtz said. "This took place during the time your class takes recess. So, let us imagine two boys from the school, oh, I don't know, let's say Patrick and Tony."

Mimi worked up a coughing jag to put the Alka-Seltzer tablet in her mouth. But Detective Kurtz was looking right at her. She had to wait for him to look away. "Why Tony and Patrick?"

Father Ernst handed Mimi a packet of photographs of them at Forest Park together, the last two showed her kissing Patrick and then kissing Tony.

"Don't you take weekends off?" she asked, handing the pictures back.

Father Ernst put the pictures down on the bench. "We've been working this case all weekend," he said. "And apparently three students were working it, too. They sneaked into the school Saturday night."

"I don't know anything about that," Mimi said.

"SOMEBODY MOVED YOUR TEACHER'S CRACKERS TO MAKE HER LOOK CUCKOO!" Detective Kurtz shouted.

Mimi and Father Ernst looked at him.

Detective Kurtz rubbed his elbow, still tender from the fall he took on the bike rack. He lowered his voice. "Let's forget about whoever broke into the school. That's just a sideshow. The main show is this mailman robbery outside your house on the day this fake letter supposedly arrived. For the two boys to wear masks shows what? It shows they wanted to conceal their identity."

"So?"

"So, for them to strip to their underwear tells me that their regular clothes would have revealed their identity. Now what type of clothes would do that?"

"Designer jeans?"

"Bullshit."

Mimi coughed up some more, and as Detective Kurtz shot Father Ernst a frustrated glance, she brought the paper towel to her mouth— pretending to spit in it—and put the crushed Alka-Seltzer on her tongue.

"We're thinking they took off their clothes because they were school uniforms," Father Ernst said gently. "They didn't want the mailman to know they go to this school."

"Mmm," Mimi said as the Alka-Seltzer began to dissolve. Powerful bubbles were stirring and stinging, generating a surge of saliva.

Detective Kurtz raised his voice again. This time his case was coming to a finish, and he wanted Mimi to squirm. "So then, the question is why are Patrick and Tony helping you with your little mailman problem? It can only be because you're helping them with the snow globe investigation. After all, stealing a snow globe and putting it on a roof is boy shit. Your shit is to make up all these lies that everybody told us. We knew it was you because you're *meticulous.* That's what gave you away, Mimi. You're too meticulous."

Spit bubbles started to form on the corners of Mimi's lips. She knew as soon as she spoke they would come lathering out even more, so she thought about what to say. But nothing came to mind. So much spit was piling up inside her mouth, she was forced to swallow. It was a chalky blend of popping crystals now dragging down the back of her throat.

"Let's make a clean confession," Father Ernst said. "Just tell us who put the snow globe on the roof and you'll feel better."

"That's right," Detective Kurtz said, lowering his tone back to a friendly balm, "you give us the boys and we'll forgive you for anything you ever did wrong. We don't want you. We want the boys who did the snow globe shit and a whole lot of other crimes around town that can't go unpunished."

Mimi rubbed her throat, keeping her mouth shut as more saliva bubbles blossomed.

"I'll tell you what," Detective Kurtz said leaning forward. He held out an ink pen to Mimi and she took it. "You don't have to say their names. Just stand up and come over here and put a little mark on this list of the class, a little mark by the names of the boys who did it. That way, it won't have come from your mouth."

Mimi stood up. She felt dizzy. She took a step forward and raised her right hand holding a shaky pen toward the paper on the desktop. The pen tip was like the nose of a distressed jetliner losing altitude, approaching a runway of boy's names. Detective Kurtz leaned forward to watch the pen tip descend.

Mimi's face was hot. The chocolate shake and two bites of a blueberry Pop Tart she had for breakfast were coming in for a landing. She tried to swallow, but instead everything came hurtling out, sloshing in a chunky puddle on the list of names, splashing up fizzy particles on Detective Kurtz's shirt and face.

"SHIT!"

"Sorry, I've gotta go," Mimi said, wiping her mouth with her arm and hurrying out the door. She dry-heaved down the hallway, zigzagging between the sports trophies and honor roll, neither of which mentioned her name, and then fainted on the floor.

CHAPTER 40

THE AMBULANCE SCREAMED outside the window in front of the school. Patrick and Tony's class leaped from their desks and ran to the window to look out as it pulled up down below. A pair of medics with a stretcher jogged up the steps.

"Everyone sit down this instant!" Miss Kleinschmidt yelled. "No one gave you permission to get up. Sit down now. Whatever's going on out there is none of our concern."

Patrick looked at Tony. They both knew it was Mimi and ran out of the class to go see. Miss Kleinschmidt shouted for them to stop, *stop this instant or else* … but they ignored her. She slammed a desk drawer shut and hobbled after them.

When Patrick and Tony got down by the principal's office, they saw Mimi on the stretcher with her face up and eyes closed. Foam was coming from her mouth. The medics trotted her past the trophy case and down the steps.

Detective Kurtz and Father Ernst stood talking with the principal and Monsignor O'Day. Monsignor O'Day was on crutches with a cast on his leg from the Spring Follies accident. Tony ran after Mimi to call out her name. But she was unconscious and didn't answer. They slid her into the ambulance like a pizza into an oven and shut the door. The ambulance sped away, siren wailing. Tony came back inside, his head down, and felt an arm grab him.

"Mister Vivamano."

It was Detective Kurtz with vomit chunks on his uniform shirt.

"What happened? Is she all right?" Tony asked.

"She's fine, just a little faint. But you're not fine. Neither is your friend." Detective Kurtz led him over to Patrick who's arm was squeezed tight in Miss Kleinschmidt's grip.

"We've solved the case," Detective Kurtz said, bluffing. "Before she got sick, Mimi told us who did it. It was these two here, Patrick and Tony."

Monsignor O'Day looked at the boys.

Sister Helen looked at the boys.

Father Ernst and Detective Kurtz looked at the boys.

This was it. Detective Kurtz knew all he had to do was say nothing. Make them believe they were already caught and under the terror of the moment they would confess.

Patrick looked at Tony. How easy it would be to rip their arms free and run down the hallway to the train tracks. If only Tony would come along.

Tony looked at Patrick. His eyes told him the whole story. He understood why Patrick had kissed Mimi. Things happen around a girl like her. Who wouldn't want to kiss her? The main thing was Tony and Patrick were best friends and that couldn't change.

Patrick's legs tingled, ready to bolt for the bridge, ready to run alongside the first freight that rumbled down the tracks, ready to escape and show the whole school that he and Tony were just as good as, and even better than, the Gang of Five who busted out for a measly few hours way back in the fifth grade. This was big time. Dillinger would be proud. They were leaving town.

Tony took a breath, ready to confess. Patrick's eyes burned. Yes, yes, yes, admit it, Tony, just say the words, just say we did it, and we can run. Just open your mouth.

Tony opened his mouth.

But before he could speak, Monsignor O'Day cut in. "All right, that's enough, this thing has gone far enough."

Everyone looked at him. He was shaking his head, leaning on his crutches and getting flush in the face. This was *his* parish and he was taking it back. "I have an announcement to make." He swung his crutches around and limped into the principal's office. Flipping a switch, he turned on the loud speaker and grabbed the microphone. Intercoms in every room on the school lit up.

Six hundred students stopped what they were doing and listened. Patrick and Tony and Detective Kurtz and Father Ernst and Miss Kleinschmidt listened from the hallway.

"Attention students, this is Monsignor O'Day. We've had a girl take sick and leave just now for the hospital in an ambulance. I want you all to pray for her." He turned to the hallway and asked the principal a question. "What's her name again?"

"Mimi Maloney," the principal said.

"Today, I want you to say a prayer for Mimi Maloney. She's riding in that ambulance all alone. Some day that will be you and me on that ride. Say a prayer for her like you mean it. Ask God to make her well."

Monsignor O'Day looked out in the hallway at Patrick, still in Miss Kleinschmidt's grip, and Tony, who was held by Detective Kurtz.

"Also today, I am announcing a general amnesty for anyone involved in the recent prank that has caused so much tension. Anyone who wants to go over to the church now to go to confession and pray, I'll be waiting there for you, ready to forgive and forget. And as always, anything you admit in confession will be a secret."

"Damn," Detective Kurtz muttered. He let go of Tony, and Miss Kleinschmidt stepped away from Patrick. "I wont forget you boys," Detective Kurtz said with a voice full of grit. "You two ever get in any other trouble outside school, I'll remember you."

"You smell like puke," Tony said stepping free of him. He went over to Patrick and hugged him.

Patrick was relieved, but also depressed. Once again, his plans to escape had been ruined. And they still had Mimi to worry about. No one knew what was wrong with her. Students started pouring out of classrooms to go over the church and pray for her. The church bells by the gold statute of Mary tolled, and Detective Kurtz and Father Ernst closed their files, got in their cars and drove away. Miss Kleinschmidt went back to her room, sat at her desk, and stuffed a soda cracker in her mouth.

CHAPTER 40

MIMI LAY IN HER hospital bed asleep with fever. An intravenous tube attached to her arm dripped saline solution into her dehydrated system. Her parents and a young nun from the hospital sat holding vigil. It was now night and the room was dark except for a reading lamp over by the best chair where Mr. Maloney sat in his work suit with a loosened tie. He and Mrs. Maloney had been there all afternoon, waiting for some word on what was wrong with their rebellious, headstrong daughter. The nun was holding her rosary beads in one hand and working a cool rag on Mimi's forehead with the other.

"She's a beautiful girl," the nun said.

"She's our baby girl," Mrs. Maloney said, running the back of a finger along Mimi's cheek.

"Maybe we should sign her up for softball, get her out of her room more," Mr. Maloney said. "That's all she needs."

The doctor came in with a clipboard of test results. Mr. and Mrs. Maloney stood up.

"You may want to sit down," he whispered.

Mrs. Maloney covered her mouth with her hand and sank into her chair, fearing news of some dreaded, incurable disease.

"Is it her adenoids?" Mr. Maloney asked, still standing.

"I'm afraid not. Your daughter is suffering from morning sickness. She's pregnant."

Mrs. Maloney gasped. The nun dropped her rosary beads. Mr. Maloney sat down with his mouth open. He looked at the floor, then looked up at the doctor.

"You sure you've got the right room?"

The doctor nodded.

Mrs. Maloney started to cry. Mr. Maloney got out a handkerchief. Mrs. Maloney reached out, thinking it was for her. But Mr. Maloney used it to blow his own nose like a trumpet blast and wadded it back up in his pocket.

"This can't be right," he said.

The nun at Mimi's side rose up slowly to let them be alone. Mimi started to mumble in her sleep with her eyes closed and they all looked over at her.

"Just three more days," she said, "three more days."

Her parents and the nun hurried to her side. Mrs. Maloney brushed back Mimi's wet bangs.

"It's okay, Mimi," she said, "Mommy and Daddy are here. It's okay."

Mimi opened her eyes. They were unfocused and bright green in the light from the reading lamp. She looked at her parents and the strange nun.

"You fainted at the school. You're at the hospital now," her mom said.

"I had a dream that I saw her."

"Who?"

"It was her."

"Who?" her mom asked.

Mimi looked to the side, remembering the spectacle of the dream. Her lips were chapped and cracked. "Mary."

The three adults looked at each other, then back at Mimi.

"Shhhh," her mom said. "It was just a dream. You need to go back to sleep and rest."

"You want some 7-Up?" her dad asked. "I'll buy you anything you want."

Mimi rubbed her eyes. "No, thanks." She looked at the nun. "Who are you?"

"I'm with the hospital."

"She was rubbing my forehead. She was on the golf course."

"Mimi, the nun was rubbing your forehead right here in this room with a cool cloth," her mother said. "You fainted at school."

"No, it was on the golf course," Mimi insisted.

"You've been under a great strain," Mr. Maloney said. "Mary wasn't on any golf course."

"But she was. She was on the golf course by the ladies tee on the fifth hole by Suicide Hill and she came out of the trees. And you know what?"

"What?" the nun asked eagerly.

"She was barefoot. Her feet were lovely."

"Honey, don't think about it," her mom said. "Just rest."

Mr. Maloney nudged the nun and whispered. "Maybe you should go tell the doctor to get a sedative."

The nun nodded in obedience, but then Mimi grabbed her by the sleeve of her habit and went on.

"I could see her face. She was sad, but very beautiful."

"Did she say anything?" the nun asked.

"Sister!" Mr. Maloney glared at the nun and whispered sharp. "Don't encourage her."

"No, it's all right," Mimi said looking at them, "I want to remember before I forget. She told me ... she was brilliant white ... she told me to—" Mimi stopped and looked at her parents. She didn't know they already knew she might be pregnant. She wanted to tell them gently, so they wouldn't be clobbered with the news. "She told me to have the baby and—"

Mr. Maloney stepped back pointing at the nun. "Now, that's enough. She can't ... no way. She's an eighth grade girl." He turned to his wife. "It's the law now. She has every right to her own future. She needs to have—"

"She told me to 'Visit Colorado and have the baby'." Mimi's voice was tired, but resolute.

"Visit Colorado and have the baby?" the nun repeated.

Mr. Maloney picked up a bowl of green Jell-O from Mimi's untouched dinner tray and threw it against the corner wall. The bowl broke and the Jell-O stuck to the wall and dribbled down to the floor in globs. He raised his voice. "This is ridiculous. It's all from that thing that happened at school. That's it. Don't you see?"

His wife and the nun and Mimi looked at him. He could see they were afraid of his outburst, so he steadied himself. "Don't you see? She's just having a bad dream, a mix-up of everything that happened at school with that statue, the statue of Mary on the church roof. She's had a shock. Mary isn't running around the golf course telling girls to visit Colorado."

"That's what she told me," Mimi whispered.

Mr. Maloney slumped down in the best chair again and covered his eyes with his hands.

Mrs. Maloney sat on the bed by Mimi's feet looking at the floor. The room was quiet for a few seconds.

The nun spoke up with nervous resolve. She knew Mr. Maloney would not like what she had to say. "The Order has a school for girls like Mimi. It's in Colorado."

Everyone looked at her.

The nun picked up the rosary off the floor and put it in her pocket. She cleared her throat and spoke calmly believing this was why she was sent. "It's outside Denver. It's a good school where girls can go in secret to have babies, to adopt them out to good families who will raise them and love them as their own. While they're there, the girls study and keep up with their classes, and when it's over, they can come home. No one need ever know."

Mrs. Maloney looked at her husband to see what he would say.

He looked like he was melting into the fabric of the chair, his voice rough and weak. "She's an eighth grade girl, dammit. She's supposed to go to school with her sister in the fall. This can't be right. I just got a promotion."

CHAPTER 41

THE LAST BELL of the last class of the last day of eighth grade finally rang. Patrick and Tony were sitting in their desks watching the clock like everyone else. The nine planets of the solar system hung in space waiting. When the big hand swept upon the top of the hour, the bell rang out and all six hundred students in the school broke into wild cheering, the eighth graders louder than all the rest of them. Just like that, it was summer. And it was over.

Some of the students got up to shake hands with Miss Kleindschmidt. She smiled and acted as if everyone had been friends all along. But Patrick and Tony kept their distance. They drifted over to Mimi's empty desk wondering how she was doing. She had missed the final few days. Her parents sent a message to the school, which Miss Kleinschmidt relayed to the class. Mimi had a strep throat and couldn't attend school or graduation. She might be contagious.

Patrick grabbed his book on Dillinger and walked across the threshold into the hallway. Tony followed. The hallway was full of kids jumping and yelling—boys with their shirttails out, girls shaking their hair wild. Jimmy Purvis had a magic marker and he asked everyone to sign the back of his good white uniform shirt. On the playground, a lot of kids stood around dazed. Birds chirped. Feathery white dandelion seeds drifted in the breeze. It was like one of those World War II movies when the POWs realize they can leave the prison camp because the Nazi's have all fled in the night and yet they don't quite know where to go.

"I'm hungry," Tony said.

So, Tony and Patrick went to Tony's house to eat the biggest after school snack ever.

Tony put on an apron and made two meatball sandwiches with extra sauce and melted cheese. He forgot to put the tray in the toaster oven and cheese dripped down on the heating element smoking up the kitchen. The smoke alarm went off and he and Patrick laughed so hard they almost cried, and then they opened the kitchen door to air out the room. They drank Vess lemon lime soda in big glasses, and put handfuls of Old Vienna potato chips on their plates. Then Tony sliced two pieces of leftover chocolate cake with ice cream on the side and they took the whole feast into the TV room to watch a full afternoon of reruns.

"We should call up Mimi to see how she's doing," Tony said.

So, Tony dialed the number and cleared his throat while it was ringing and fixed his hair a little.

"There's no answer," he said after about fifteen rings. He hung up and they went back into the TV room to watch the *Twilight Zone*. It was the episode in which a man and woman find themselves in a strange town with no other people, and in the end they find out they're in a girl's play village on another planet. They had been taken in the night while driving home.

"Do you think she'll go to the graduation?" Tony asked.

"I don't know. I hope so."

They both wanted to hear everything about Mimi's final interrogation and what she said to make the authorities give up. Sometimes girls would tease the boys by saying girls were smarter than boys. And now Patrick and Tony were convinced. Mimi was the very embodiment of that saying, and they both wanted to let her know she had done a great job with the investigation.

Tony's older brother came home from his last day of freshman year at St. Aloysius. He plopped down a big pile of books he was planning to read over the summer and had a light snack to send essential nutrients straight to his brain cells.

"What are you shitheads doing?" he asked, looking at their mess of plates and their lazy bodies rolled out on the couch and floor before the TV.

"Gimmie a break, it's summer," Tony said.

Tony's brother drank his protein drink and went upstairs to lift weights. He had a whole plan for the summer to make money and get ready for the fall.

"What are we gonna do this summer?" Tony asked.

"Is it really summer? Did we really just leave grade school forever?"

"Hell, yeah."

They got out the BB gun and shot some soda cans in the backyard and had a cigarette behind the garage and enjoyed the afternoon with nothing on their agenda except the graduation ceremony Saturday night.

Chapter 42

ON SATURDAY MORNING, Sister Mathilda hoisted her suitcase from her bed and walked out of her room at the nunnery. It was time to depart for the retirement home. A line of nuns along the walkway outside hugged and kissed her in the sunlight. She was the last nun still wearing the black habit at Mary Queen of Our Hearts, and on this day she had put on a fresh, clean habit for the trip. The nuns gave her a card and a box of candy and thanked her for all she had done.

"Thirty-two years," she told them. "It went fast." Then she swallowed back a sigh looking over at the school, knowing she would never go inside to teach again. Her students from all those years, thousands of them, were now grown adults, working in offices and raising families. None came to thank her or bid her farewell. Her exit was like a private burial with immediate family only.

"Here come the boys," the principal said.

Father Maligan's car drove up the playground from the priests' house. He parked it and Monsignor O'Day got out on crutches.

"What's this all about? Are you running away?" Monsignor said.

Sister Mathilda nodded at the joke, the last joke she would ever hear from Monsignor O'Day. He limped over on his crutches, while Father Maligan hung back to pick his nose succinctly.

"No foolin', we're gonna miss you," Monsignor O'Day said. He gave her a hug and looked her in the eyes. She had no tears. Her eyes were calm and ready to go. "Something for you to remember us by," Monsignor said. He turned to Father Maligan who was walking up with a gift in his hand. It was a portrait-sized picture wrapped in funny papers from that morning.

"What is this, a picture of you?" she joked.

"Even better. Something to remember us by," Monsignor O'Day said.

This was one of his favorite possessions, which he had taken from his own bedroom wall and wrapped in the morning funny papers for her. She opened it. It was a photograph of the school and church taken from a helicopter, showing the playground as a muddy field with construction equipment. On a flatbed truck was the gold statue of Mary next to a crane ready to lift her to the roof.

Sister Mathilda held it to her chest. "Thank you, Monsignor. I will take good care of it, and now I can see it. I can see everything now."

Father Maligan ambled up. "One more thing, you bird." He reached in his pocket and pulled out a folded up piece of paper. She opened it up. It was the program from the night Father Maligan had taken her to the racetrack. "Just so you don't forget me and all the fun we had."

Some of the younger nuns looked over and saw the picture of a racehorse on the front. Sister Mathilda thanked him and gave him a hug.

"Well, be sure to write and let us know how the food is," Monsignor O'Day said. "It can't be any worse than here."

A new nun in modern clothes took her suitcase and put it in the trunk of the principal's car. Sister Helen got behind the wheel and Sister Mathilda got in the passenger side. Everyone lined up to wave and watch her pull away, and then she was gone.

"Some day, that'll be us," Monsignor O'Day said to Father Maligan.

Father Maligan grunted in agreement.

Sister Mathilda boarded a passenger train at the Kirkwood station after one more hug from Sister Helen. "You'll never be forgotten," the principal said.

"Yes I will. We all will. There'll be new kids, new teachers, even a new principal someday. We'll all be forgotten. And that's okay."

The train pulled away and Sister Mathilda sat by a window watching the suburbs turn to farmland. Barns and cows, rivers and fields. She looked around the train car at the other passengers—a boy with a comic book, a man with a stock page, a couple on their honeymoon just getting started. She got out the picture of the school and looked at it, then looked out the window some more at the clouds and laid her head back on the seat cushion and took a nap.

CHAPTER 43

TONY TOOK A HOT SHOWER and shaved. It was graduation night. He splashed on some of his big brother's Old Spice aftershave, and put on a clean shirt with stiff wide collars. This was a night for tight jeans and the horse head belt buckle. A night for dancing. He turned on the radio and thought of Mimi as Stevie Wonder sang "You are the Sunshine of My Life." Tony looked in the mirror and combed his thick black hair as he sang along.

His parents drove him to the gym. They sat in the metal folding chairs with the other parents. Sister Helen gave a speech about how proud she was of them and how they should do something important with their futures. Then they got their diplomas, one at a time, each student shaking hands with her and Monsignor O'Day, who sat in a chair with his leg in a cast. Afterwards, Monsignor had every kid in the graduating class sign his cast— except Mimi. She didn't show up.

"If she's sick, she's sick," Patrick said. "You'll see her over the summer."

Tony looked around at the girls. "It's been a bad year for love."

When the party started, the parents went home and the students cleared away the folding chairs and slid them on racks under the stage. It was time to eat pizza and drink soda and dance to the music. A stereo record player with 45s played the hits.

Tony unbuttoned his shirt's top two buttons to show his chest and got out on the dance floor. He put a lot of leg and shoulder muscles into his dancing. At first, he danced by himself, with his eyes closed, pretending Mimi was with him. But his moves were so heartfelt, that all the girls began to dance around him. Or maybe it was the aftershave.

"Hey, Tony, you wanna dance?"

It was Sara Jibbs, a girl who never did anything wrong.

"Sure." Tony danced with her, then he danced with Molly Lane, Ann Bennett, Janet Fowler, Susan McGregor, Elaine Moore and all through the class roster. He got around to a slow dance with Charlotte Hester to the song "My Love." Tony was doing all right.

Patrick went outside on the gym steps and sat at the bottom to have a cigarette. He tapped the end of the fresh pack of Camel non-filters that Tony had given him as a graduation present.

So this was it, he thought. Like Dillinger, the last night around the old rock pile. The night air was warm and the trees danced with the breeze. It would have been a good night to hop a train going somewhere with Tony. But that whole plan had lost its glow. He knew now he was never going to get away like that. His parents were just too immature and wouldn't be able to take it. They had gone to his graduation and hugged him and said they were proud of him. He was stuck living with them to make them happy, because they had loved him too much for him to get out of their clutches without feeling guilty. It also would have wrecked things for his brothers and sisters, because they'd be worrying all the time that he was dead, and he couldn't have proper fun on the road if he knew they were back home on their knees praying for him before they went to bed. The whole dream was stupid anyway, maybe. Maybe he only wanted to run away to rattle Miss Kleinschmidt and outshine the Gang of Five. Now that he was done with grade school, he felt lazy about the project. Besides, his bedroom had air conditioning and clean sheets.

He pulled the red strip on the pack of Camels to take off the cellophane wrapper when he heard a bike bell. He looked up and saw Mimi ride into view on her green Schwinn with the white basket. She rode up in jeans, and a fresh white t-shirt. Her hair was in a ponytail under a red Cardinals ball cap. She was chewing a big wad of bubble gum.

"Hey, you bird," she said imitating Father Maligan's voice. She wanted to get off the bike and hug him, but she stayed on the seat.

"Hey," Patrick said standing up. He wanted to hug her, but he knew Tony loved her.

Tony was inside the gym slow dancing with Charlotte Hester wishing she were Mimi.

"I heard you're real sick. You got the strep throat?" Patrick asked.

Mimi faked a cough and nodded. "I'm getting a little better." She blew a bubble and then a bubble within a bubble to avoid having to talk. It popped in her face and she peeled it off with a laugh.

"Hey, what happened with the investigation?" Patrick asked.

"Oh, they had me beat."

"Really?"

She took an honest breath. "Yeah, they figured it all out. At least that cop did, what's his name."

"Kurtz."

"Yeah, Detective Kurtz. He had me cornered and guessed pretty much the whole thing, but then I got sick and next thing I knew I woke up in the hospital."

Patrick patted her on the back. "Well, you did great! Me and Tony really wanted to tell you. We owe you."

"Thanks."

"Hey, wait here, I'll go get Tony."

"No, wait," she said.

Patrick looked at her. She gripped the handlebars and twisted her hands on them over and over again. "I have to go."

"What, are you not feeling well?"

"No, I just don't want to cry." Her voice cracked on the word "cry," so she chewed her gum a lot to cover for it.

"That's OK, we'll see you over the summer at the pool and places."

She nodded her head, as if that were true, and pulled her ball cap brim down tight on her head. Then she decided to tell him the truth. "I have to go away."

"Go away?"

"Yeah."

"Why?"

"I got accepted to a private school." So, not the whole truth, but still as much as her parents said she could tell.

"I thought you were going to Holy Footsteps."

"No, this is even better. It's run by nuns, but it's in the country where it's quiet and you can go on long walks and have time to think about everything."

Patrick scrunched up his face. "What the hell are talking about? Think about what?"

She looked around at the dumpster and the empty playground and the gleaming statue of Mary. "Oh, I don't know. Just think about, you know, the things of the Lord."

"Holy shit, Mimi, you aren't thinking about becoming—"

"A nun? No, no," she said whipping off her baseball cap and putting it back on tighter, "But this is just like a finishing school where they help you to get to know God better."

"Bullshit, Mimi, are you kidding me?" Patrick started laughing. "I thought you were serious for a minute." He kept on laughing, but noticed she wasn't laughing, so he stopped. "You're serious?"

"Yes."

"Well, where is this damned place?"

"It's not around here. It's out of state." She thought of Miss Kleinschmidt's Visit Colorado snow globe and bit back her tears.

"Oh. When are you going?"

"Tomorrow."

"Tomorrow?" Patrick slapped his forehead and looked at her. "Why so damned fast? It's barely even summer."

Patrick could see that her lashes were wet, that she'd been crying, and he had to stop himself from hugging her.

She saw him studying her face, so she put a foot on one of the pedals and got ready to shove off. "Please tell Tony I'm sorry for not going in, but I don't want him kissing me and getting sick. And I can't be kissing you, either."

Patrick nodded. "OK, but don't leave yet. Here, you want a smoke?"

"No, that shit's bad for you. You should give it up." She smiled at him and pushed off. Patrick watched her. She did a little loop around the playground ringing her bike bell as if she were still a girl at recess with nothing to worry about but homework.

Patrick tried to understand it, but he couldn't. *What the hell?* Something invisible had happened. The grade school from which Mimi had almost escaped as herself, had grabbed her at the last minute and somehow changed her. It seemed the things she had mocked—the statues and creeds—she had now ingested whole. Something awful had happened. A switch had flipped, and Mimi's gears that had been all turning one way, were now in reverse. She was no longer her own girl. She had dropped dead somehow and come back a stranger. *Mimi, Mimi ... wake up. What is your problem? What are you thinking?*

Patrick spit on the playground. Look at her, both hands on the handlebars. So proper. *Finishing school!* What a waste. She would probably end up married to a parish man with wingtips and careful ties who would work downtown, and they would send their kids to a school just like Mary Queen of Our Hearts, maybe here or in another state, and her kids would never know the truth—the *real* Mimi she had once been. They would only know her as a Catholic mom taking them to Mass on time, or ironing their school uniforms, and telling them to grow up right.

He watched as she looped around the playground once more and slipped between the church and the school, disappearing into the night. He lit his Camel and took a long drag. It was a dangerous time to be alive, the last two weeks of eighth grade. Anything could happen.

CHAPTER 44

THE GOLF CART sat in the middle of the fairway in the cool of the summer morning. Monsignor O'Day was behind the wheel with Father Maligan riding shotgun, Sister Helen and Miss Kleinschmidt were in back. It was the parish scramble fundraiser, and everyone was discussing President Nixon and whether or not he was guilty of more than he had admitted.

"I hope they send him to prison," Miss Kleinschmidt said, as she got out to hit her ball. She squinted at the flag on the green in the distance. "He's set a bad example for today's youth. Why, when I first voted for Roosevelt—"

"Stop making speeches and hit the ball, you bird," Father Maligan interrupted.

Miss Kleinschmidt got into position and took a practice swing. She was glad it was a scramble as her balls were always landing in the woods or sand traps. She told herself to pretend the pond wasn't there and hit straight for the green. The morning wind ruffled her grey hair as she swung back. With a fierce twitch forward, her club topped the ball, sending it bulleting straight into the pond where it torpedoed to the bottom, striking the leaf-covered skin of Mr. Maloney's missing hand grenade. The surface of the pond barfed up in a twenty-foot tall column of water, and Miss Kleinschmidt was blown back on her ass cursing and flailing as a bluegill landed on her blouse flopping in the sun.

"What the hell?" She flung the fish off her and scrambled to her feet.

They watched the pond waves ripple to the shore and then back again.

"What the hell kind of ball were you hitting?" Father Maligan asked.

"It wasn't the ball, you fool. There's something wrong with that pond. We should report this to the police."

She looked at Sister Helen. Sister Helen and Father Maligan looked at Monsignor O'Day.

"We aren't reporting anything," he said shaking his head, "We've had enough folly for one spring."

They got back in the golf cart and played the rest of the course as if nothing ever happened. But Miss Kleinschmidt was sullen, knowing it had something to do with the reckless boys in the parish, maybe even some boy in her own class—or even that Mimi Maloney—but some things you just can't ever prove.

ABOUT THE AUTHOR

When he's not writing, Kevin Killeen pretends to work as a reporter for KMOX Radio in St. Louis, covering crime, politics, and odd happenings of no consequence. His hobbies include tripping over his children's shoes, turning down loud music, and rubbing his wife's feet while she lies on the living room couch discussing the bills as he stares at the cracks in the ceiling. His first novel, *Never Hug a Nun* (Blank Slate Press, 2012), features the earlier exploits of Patrick Cantwell, set in Webster Groves, Missouri. It won a Ben Franklin award in the humor category from the Independent Book Publishers Association of America. His second novel, *Try to Kiss a Girl* (Blank Slate Press, 2014), featured Patrick and his family on vacation in Michigan and won the humor category in the Midwest Independent Publisher's Association's awards in 2014.

CPSIA information can be obtained at www.ICGtesting.com
Printed in the USA
LVOW10s0307291115

464300LV00004B/6/P